JOYFUL SPIRIT

Fiction for horse lovers by Barbara Morgenroth

Bittersweet Farm 1: Mounted
Bittersweet Farm 2: Joyful Spirit
Bittersweet Farm 3: Wingspread
Bittersweet Farm 4: Counterpoint
Bittersweet Farm 5: Calling all Comets

If Wishes Were Horses ~ a novella

Middle-grade horse fiction:

Dream Horse
Summer Horse

BITTERSWEET FARM 2

JOYFUL SPIRIT

Barbara Morgenroth

DASHINGBOOKS

ISBN 978-0-6158884-1-5

Cover photo by Sommer Wilson
Published by DashingBooks
Text set in Adobe Garamond

1

I BANGED ON THE DOOR AGAIN. "Lockie!"

"Shhh," Greer hissed from inside.

Seeing no point in staying longer, I turned, went down the stairs and into the barn. CB was poking his nose out between the bars again and I gave him a quick kiss as I passed by. Butch was eating the second cutting hay that we had just gotten in and it looked delicious.

As I left the barn, Lockie was getting out of his truck.

"Hi." He was smiling.

"Hi." I was not smiling.

"What's wrong?" he asked closing the truck door.

Even though it was ridiculous, I was too annoyed to find any humor in it. "You're upstairs in bed with Greer."

"Am I enjoying myself?"

"By the sound of it, very much."

"Go Lockie!" He grinned.

"I'm going to kill her," I said.

I had put up with so much from my half-sister over the years and never bothered to react but that seemed to have been my mistake. Ignoring her only upped the ante for the next time.

"No, let's go see what stunt she's pulling." Lockie grabbed my hand and ran me through the barn to the stairs to his apartment. There he brought me to a stop and whispered "You stomp up the stairs, and I'll be quiet."

I shrugged and thumped up the stairs with Lockie following me, then raised my hands questioning what was supposed to happen next. He banged on the door and motioned to me.

"Lockie! What are you doing in there?"

"Don't get up!" Greer said from inside the apartment.

Lockie started to laugh silently and motioned for me to keep going.

"If I ever get a hold of you," I said, "you're going from King Stud to Wimpy Gelding!"

"Yikes!" Lockie mouthed silently.

"You think I'm kidding? Without anesthesia!"

"Don't pay any attention to her. Talia's a coward," Greer said. "She never does anything."

"Barehanded. And if you survive that, I'm telling everyone on the east coast show circuit who castrated you and why! I'll probably get a medal!"

Leaning over to me, Lockie whispered into my ear. "Isn't that a little over the top?"

"I thought you wanted it to sound convincing!" I whispered back.

Noiselessly, Lockie went down the stairs while I stamped down behind him in a feigned rage.

As I reached the ground floor, he pushed me up against the tack room wall with his body. It was fantastic. It made up for everything.

"Tell me the truth, Silly Filly. Did you believe for one second I was in there?"

"Not for one second."

"A half a second?"

His nose was on my nose.

"No, Lockie."

I was about to kiss him when he stepped back.

"Tack CB. We'll go for that hack. I had an idea."

"Apparently that idea doesn't include me treating you like Butch," I called to him as Lockie walked toward Wing's stall.

"How so?" He picked up Wing's halter and opened the stall door.

"I would have kissed him," I said.

"You can kiss me some other time."

I stood in the middle of the aisle. "You're impossible."

"I'm very possible."

* * *

Ten minutes later, we were riding through the field that bordered the outdoor arena. In another hour, the horses would be turned out to spend the night at pasture, absent the heat and flies. In another two weeks, the fall school semester would begin. It was our senior year and while I had been indifferent before, that had changed.

It was true that The Briar School was in town. Greer and I were day students while most of our classmates lived on campus; we didn't leave home but now I didn't want to leave at all. There was so much for me to do at the barn that I wasn't sure how to get it all in after the school day.

For the first time, I wanted to take lessons. I had always loved riding but the rest of it wasn't fun. It wasn't a challenge and I wasn't engaged. That had changed because there was so much to learn from Lockie.

Instead of just a place to live, the farm now felt like home.

"This is where the cross-country course should be," Lockie said pointing toward a curve in the hill. "We can take advantage of the natural terrain."

Since the subject of an outside course hadn't been mentioned in weeks, I didn't realize he was still thinking about it.

"It won't be as demanding as some courses," he said

"Like those with a ditch and a berm," I said over him.

"I don't remember that," Lockie replied.

Lockie's memory of the fall he'd taken at that jump in the combined training event was gone and maybe that was just as well, but the after-effects remained. The headaches were persistent and the doctors my father had found for him hadn't been able to completely resolve that issue yet. I was sure there were days it hurt Lockie just to walk. His sensitivity to light was controlled, to a large degree, with special contact lenses but sounds were more acute to him than they were to me and there was nothing to be done about that.

Never complaining, Lockie managed the barn, trained horses, gave lessons, didn't ask for a pass when he didn't feel well and never lost his temper with Greer when even a saint would have been swearing at her.

Lockie reminded me so much of my mother, I had come to admire Lockie as had my father and he was a tough man to please. I saw first-hand how difficult life had been for my mother during her illness and thought Lockie possessed the same kind of stoicism she had.

I just wished he wouldn't take the chances he did on his horse. The doctors didn't want him to ride at the same level he had previously, but riding was his life and it wasn't something Lockie was going to give up easily or at all. Training horses and coaching riders wasn't enough.

While understanding his desire to continue riding, I knew it was so easy to take a fall. The last time I hit the ground, it had been over nothing. Butch shied and I hadn't been paying attention so my legs weren't tight on the saddle. Off I went.

The same thing could happen to Lockie, too. A moment's distraction, leaves blowing, or a squirrel running in front of Wing could be the cause. It didn't have to be over a huge fence and the truth was that Lockie couldn't afford to hit the ground again.

"Talia. Are you paying attention?" Lockie said.

"I thought you gave up on the idea of having an outside course. Greer does all her jumping in the ring and I'm not . . ."

"Yeah, I know and I wanted to talk to you about that."

"What?" I felt a rush of impending doom.

"There's a hunter pace in late September and I would like you and Rogers to ride it."

"No."

"Why not?"

"I'm done competing."

"It's not competing. It's like hacking through the woods with your friend."

"Since other teams will also be riding and there's a time element, I think that could be categorized as a competition."

"If you're going to nitpick . . ."

"Why should I ride it?"

"Because I can't and Rogers needs the experience on Karneval."

As good a friend as Rogers might be, and while I wished her well on the horse she had bought from us, this wasn't sufficient motivation to convince me to compete.

"That's not a good enough reason, sorry. Find someone else."

"It should be a team from Bittersweet."

"Why?"

"Because your father asked me to get the farm's name in the paper once in a while. I couldn't get Greer to the National Horse Show, so . . ."

"That's not your fault!" I said over him.

"I don't know when Greer's first show success will be. This will be good for everyone."

"Except me."

"All right."

"You're going to leave it at that?" I asked.

"I told you I'm not here to make you miserable."

"And you're okay with me saying no?"

"If you don't want to, you don't want to."

We kept riding up the hill.

"I'll do it," Lockie added.

"That's so unfair!" I should have known there was a trap in it for me.

"No, it's not. I want to do it and you don't."

"Your doctors don't want you to compete," I reminded him.

Lockie turned in the saddle. "It's not competing, it's just riding across country like we are now."

"We're not galloping!"

"Because we're talking."

"Not anymore." I turned CB around and cantered down the hill away from him. A moment later Lockie was galloping beside us, leaving me no choice but to pull up.

"What are you doing?" I demanded.

"I'm trying to talk to you."

"You galloped down the hill!"

"I'm not going to live in bubble wrap for the rest of my life. I'm sorry if that upsets you. Stop worrying and enjoy my life with me."

"I actually do understand this," I began.

"Good."

"Let me finish. You love riding, but it's not worth risking your life. Be grateful. If that means having to give up some things, then you do that. You were blessed and it seems like you don't appreciate it."

"Maybe by living my life fully that expresses my appreciation," Lockie replied.

I was so angry with him I couldn't say another word. After untacking CB, I returned him to his stall and going up to the house went directly to my father's office.

I tapped on the door.

"Come on," he said.

I entered to find him on the phone.

"I'll call you back. Bye." He hung up. "Hi, Talia. What's wrong?"

I was so transparent that everyone who looked at me apparently could detect exactly how I felt? Terrific. I paced to the bookshelf then back to the window.

"What happened?" He asked.

"Lockie," I managed to say.

"Is he okay?"

"He won't be if he keeps taking chances!"

"Would you like to sit down?"

"No."

"All right. What did he do?"

"The doctors said . . ." I couldn't finish.

My father waited for a moment.

"He . . ."

"I loved your mother. Watching her fade and not be able to do anything drove me crazy. It was the first time in my life that I was so ineffective."

"Tell Lockie . . ."

"No, it doesn't work that way."

"Dad!"

My father smiled. "You almost sound like Greer."

"No, I don't."

My father picked up his phone and keyed in some numbers. "You'll talk to Lockie's doctor. Ask the doctor the question you fear most."

"Dad," I began to protest.

"Ask. Get past it. Say the words. Say 'Is he going to die from the injuries he sustained in the accident?'"

I glared at him.

"That's what you want to know, isn't it?"

I didn't respond because the answer was yes and we both knew it.

"Hi," he said into the phone. "This is Andrew Swope. Is Dr. Jarosz available? Thank you." He held out the phone to me. "After you talk, I want you to take a shower, put on something nice, and we'll all have dinner."

2

SITTING ON THE FLOOR of the shower stall, I cried as the water streamed over me. Years of tears in a seemingly endless flow poured out. When I was spent, I stood, turned off the water and got ready for dinner.

"Good," my father said as I entered the dining room.

Lockie was already seated at the foot of the table with Jules, our live-in chef and my confidant, who was seated across from my place. I sat.

Greer had driven off earlier while Lockie and I were out in the field. Maybe she was embarrassed or maybe she didn't give a damn when she saw his truck parked in front of the barn. Maybe she thought that hurting me was all that mattered.

"Before we have dinner," my father said, "I'm going to speak and you two will listen."

I didn't look up from my salad plate.

"I understand how passionately you both hold your positions and that's admirable. Tali, your concern for Lockie is an expression of one of your finer qualities. You possess a deep capacity for compassion. It's something you inherited from your mother." He paused. "But, undoubtedly, not from me."

I took a sip of water.

"Lockie, riding is your life," my father continued. "It could also shorten your life. We like you very much so we would prefer it if you were with us for as long as possible. What to do? What to do with you two."

"Tell him what the doctors told him," I interjected. "He's not supposed to ride."

"They didn't say that," Lockie replied. "They said I could ride."

"You take too many chances," I said.

"I had one bad fall in fifteen years of riding. How do you know that will ever happen again?"

"It doesn't have to be the same, all it has to be is a fall," I shot back. "Dad?"

"I can't live a half-life," Lockie said.

"It's better to be alive." The words almost tasted as bitter as they sounded.

"Time out," my father said. "Talia, you said you trusted me to help Lockie."

I looked at him. I had never been fair to him and this question made me realize that. In some stupid way for me, he was entangled with the loss of my mother. She had loved him and he had also been the source of her own emotional pain. Too young to understand the relationship they had, all I could see was her sadness and blamed him for it.

Normal families consisted of a father, mother, and children living in the same house. I didn't have that. Many of my classmates didn't either, but that wasn't foremost in my mind. There was another family, Greer's, and adult complications that were beyond a child. All I could see was that my parents weren't together and it was a source of distress for my mother. When she became ill, somehow the two issues were conflated. In my nine year old mind, someone needed to be responsible and I chose him.

"It's a bad habit of mine," I replied.

"She's upset," Lockie said.

"Please don't make excuses for my bad behavior," I said to him. "But I'm not going to stop worrying about you."

"It's unnecessary," Lockie replied.

"I thought this was my turn to speak," my father said.

"I apologize," I told him, wanting only to get up from the table and stay in my bedroom for a couple days.

My father pointed to me. "You will get off Lockie's

case." He pointed to Lockie. "You will stop taking chances."

I was reluctant to say anything. It didn't seem like much of a resolution to the situation. I was supposed to stop worrying about Lockie and what constituted "taking chances"? That could be anything from a trail ride to the hunter pace.

"From your expressions, I see that displeases both of you. Good."

My father was enjoying this all too much. "That means my dictum weighs equally."

"Is it time for dinner?" Jules asked.

"Not quite. I have news. Talia asked me to do something for her some weeks ago."

"And you found the doctors for Lockie," I replied.

"Yes. After I discussed Lockie's status with Dr. Jarosz, I realized he wouldn't want to give up riding no matter what the doctors said. In fact, it would be wiser if you didn't ride again, Lockie, but since that's not your chosen path, we have to work with you. The problem is not hitting the ground or even hitting your head. A helmet will protect a rider's head from a rock but it doesn't do enough to minimize what happens when the impact causes the rider's brain to hit the inside of the skull. Brain against bone is not an optimal event."

"I was wearing the best helmet available."

"They're good but we're going to do better. We're developing a new helmet. The force of the impact must be absorbed before it reaches the brain."

I looked at Jules and she smiled encouragingly at me. At that moment, I fell in love with my father and was certain, beyond doubt, that this is the man my mother had loved.

"That's possible?" Lockie asked.

"Yes."

I turned to Lockie then back to my father.

My father smiled. "I went to a helmet manufacturer and brought a composite material designed for some other application entirely and asked them to put the two together. We'll have a prototype soon. Until then, I would ask you, Lockie, to limit your riding to what the doctors have prescribed. When we have the new helmet and are sure that it works as we hope, then perhaps we can convince the doctors to give you more leeway on your activities."

"Agreed," Lockie replied.

"And you, Talia?" my father asked me.

"Yes, of course."

"Good. If only everything was so easy to negotiate," my father said as he picked up his fork.

There was silence at the table for a moment.

"Is there anything, in some small measure, I can do to repay you," Lockie asked.

Jules' fork, dropping on her plate a little too hard, made me glance in her direction. Pushing her chair back, she stood. "Excuse me," Jules said and hurried from the room.

My father stood and moved away from the table. "Excuse me. Carry on with dinner," he said as he followed her out.

Lockie turned to me. "Why is Jules starting to cry? What did I say?"

"Jules is very fond of you."

"Does that have another meaning?"

"No." Starting on my salad, then I stopped. "I think she was touched by your offer."

"Why aren't you crying?"

"I don't have any tears left after our disagreement."

Lockie moved his plate away. "I told you I wasn't here to make you miserable and by being here I've done it just that."

"It's so much more complicated than that." I reached for his plate and put it back in front of him. "Eat, please."

Lockie didn't pick up his fork.

"All I ever wanted to do was ride," Lockie paused, then began again. "When I was young, there was a riding academy near my home. After school, I would ride my bicycle to the stable. From the road, I would watch the riders. We didn't have money for lessons, and even if we did, my father would have thought it was a waste.

"One day while I was watching, the owner stopped his pickup truck next to me. He said he had seen me as I stared at these children my age, these fortunate children who had no idea how lucky they were to have the lessons and the boots and the special pants. I didn't know what they were called until I read about them in a book in the school library. Jodhpurs. From India. It was such an exotic word and so removed from my circumstances.

"He asked what I was doing. I didn't know how to answer. It was as if I was seeing performances by characters from a storybook, alien and unreal. There was such unimaginable beauty in becoming one with a horse and it was so unattainable for me."

I was wrong. There were tears left.

"Don't cry, Tali," Lockie said. "There's a happy ending. He told me I could come into the barnyard and watch from there. I went every day and couldn't take my eyes off the horses and riders. He began letting me help, and, in a few weeks, persuaded my father to allow me work there. I was about eight and wasn't much of a stablehand but I tried. On the day Ed put me on a pony, I felt my life made sense for the first time.

"After the accident, my life wasn't right for a long while. Then I came here."

"To the farm I couldn't wait to leave." I shook my head at the irony of our lives converging here.

"Your father is a very generous man."

"My father is someone I don't even know," I replied.

"We'll get Tracy to ride with Rogers on the hunter pace and I'll try not to give either of you cause to be concerned for me again."

Tracy was a local young woman who had worked with us for about two years and she was very reliable but I thought for her first time out of Karneval, Rogers would want me instead of someone she barely knew.

"I'll ride with Rogers."

"You've been blessed in your life. I know you don't feel that, but there are so few things asked of you, don't do something you don't want to do when it makes no difference."

"You were right to call me a spoiled brat."

"That day? We were just pretending for Greer's benefit."

"You're describing someone who is both incredibly spoiled and incredibly ungrateful. I feel like Greer. In my worst nightmare, I don't want to be like her."

"You're not."

I wasn't sure of that.

* * *

Late that night I was reading the second book of the evening in bed when my phone rang.

It was Lockie.

"Go to sleep, Talia."

* * *

The next morning I tapped on my father's library door.

"Come in."

I entered carefully since there was a mug of coffee in my

hand. Crossing the room, I placed it on a pad on his desk and he looked at me, caught off-guard.

"Good morning, Tali. What's up?"

"I was awake for a long time last night and I'd like to discuss a couple things with you."

He closed the lid to his laptop. "Okay."

"I want to stay home."

"You are home."

"I want to stay home full time and I would like it if you would be here more often."

"I don't understand."

"I don't want to go to college."

"I don't blame you but you haven't graduated from high school yet."

"I don't want to do that either."

"That's not negotiable."

"I'll take a GED and be done with it."

"Why?"

I paused.

"Is it about Lockie? You spoke to the doctor. He's in good health and everything is being managed. You don't need to become his guardian the way you did for your mother. You don't have to take that on. You didn't need to take it on the last time."

"I know that but my mother's passing made a big impression on me."

"The wrong one," he replied.

"No, it's the right one. I want to be with the people I care about."

He looked at me in surprise. "And that's why you want me to stay home more often?"

"Yes."

"School is in town. It's six hours a day. Maybe your schedule can be shortened by taking only the classes you need to graduate."

I shook my head.

My father nodded. "You know what your grandfather says."

"Always sleep on it before making an important decision."

"Let's give it some time. We'll both think about it."

* * *

Pushing two wheelbarrows, we walked through the field up the hill to drive stakes in the ground where Lockie wanted jumps built by the crew who did construction at the farm. I knew he had spent hours designing the course, drawing the jumps and giving specifics regarding size. It had been explained to me that the course was customizable in that it could be made more difficult later, but this first version was entry level. There were no water jumps, and no obstacles that would intimidate horse or rider.

I thought the jump that looked like a futon was insane but wasn't going to say anything about it.

"You told me a story about having a fall over a fence some years ago as the reason why you aren't keen on jumping," Lockie said as we continued up the hill.

"It's a true story, completely autobiographical."

"Why don't you want to show?"

"Why do you want to?"

"I enjoy competition. It's a gauge to determine how the training is progressing," Lockie explained.

"Why can't you just ride for the fun of it?"

"This is a business. My job is to turn out capable horses and capable riders, not Sunday hacks and hobbyists."

"Horses don't want to do this. They have nothing to gain. They would prefer to be in a field eating all day."

"Are you kidding me?"

"No, I'm serious," I said.

"Do you think you could force CB to jump anything he didn't want to?"

"Maybe I couldn't but you could."

Lockie laughed. "No, I couldn't. I've ridden horses that couldn't be forced into anything. Have you ever seen a horse that wouldn't get in a trailer? They tell you in a hundred ways when they don't want to do the work whether it's balking at jumps or smaller rebellions like kicking you or biting at you. They can simply refuse to move."

"Then leave them alone," I said.

"It's self-selecting. The horses who don't want to work,

wind up not working and we don't have to be more descriptive than that.

"Most horses want to do something. Bored horses pace in their stalls or chew on the pasture fence. You said yourself that CB has a swish he does when he seems pleased with himself."

"That's true."

"If he can be pleased with himself, he must enjoy the work. So if it's not about CB, it must be about you."

We stopped at the next location where Lockie had requested telephone poles be stacked in a pyramid shape. The height could be increased with a couple rails placed above the base.

"Is this what you meant when you said you should have become a psychiatrist?"

"Tali, we're going to be spending a lot of time together. Maybe I'd like to know what's going on with you."

"It's not coming from dark psychological depths," I replied stepping on one of the fiberglass posts and driving it into the ground. "I don't want to be judged."

"It's not personal."

"For you it's not. For me, I grew up feeling as though my mother and I were somehow not good enough for my father to be with us fulltime."

Lockie looked at me in surprise.

"It doesn't have to make sense. It's the logic of a child."

"You're not a child anymore."

"Some of these emotional injuries are not so easily over-come."

"I hope I've never said or done anything to make you feel . . ."

"No, you haven't. Don't give it another thought."

It was hitting too close to home already.

3

THE NEXT MORNING when I came down for breakfast, I was surprised to find my father there waiting for me.

"Hi."

"I have an answer for you," he said. "It was, surprisingly, both difficult and simple since I want you to have whatever you want but I also feel obligated to do what your mother would wish me to do for you."

I sat.

"You can stay home."

"Wonderful."

"Maybe so. You'll work harder than you can dream possible. You'll have a tutor and you'll learn everything your mother would want you to know, then you'll begin doing work for the foundation. And Jules will also teach you how to cook."

He looked at me expectantly.

"And you will be where?"

"I will be here making sure this happens."

"Can I choose my own hours?"

"As long as you get the work done, yes."

"Then it sounds perfect."

"What's perfect," Greer asked coming into the room.

"I'm not going back to The Briar School."

Reaching over my shoulder, Greer grabbed a croissant from the basket on the table. "Good. Where are you going?"

"I'm staying home."

"Drop-out," Greer said with a smile as she sat down next to Jules.

"No, I'm going to have a tutor."

Greer poured herself a cup of coffee. "So it's too hard to maintain the illusion of being socially viable. I don't blame you. If my boyfriend was gay, I'd stay home, too." She sipped the coffee. "What is this swill?"

"Jamaican Blue Mountain," Jules replied.

"Ugh."

Greer spread some preserves on her croissant then choked. "What's this?"

"White peach and lemon verbena."

"Why can't we have normal food?" Greer demanded and pushed back from the table.

"I'll make you normal food from now on if you give me twelve hours' notice that you'll be present," Jules replied.

"Dad," my sister snapped. "Is this how you let the help speak to us?"

"Shut up, Greer," I said.

My father reached for another croissant. "You're the only one complaining, Greer, if you would take the time to notice."

"Maybe I'm the only one with high standards."

We all looked at her.

"What?"

"Why don't you go warm up Counterpoint? I'll be at the barn in a few minutes," Lockie said to her.

"I was planning to go shopping this morning."

"I only have an hour free today," Lockie replied.

Ignoring him, Greer turned to our father. "Am I supposed to be at his beck and call?"

"There's a crew coming to begin working on the outside course. Lockie will be engaged with that," my father replied finishing his coffee.

"If you want to go to the schooling show in two weeks, you better ride your horse."

"Schooling show? Like I'm a beginner?"

I wanted to throw something at her but the only thing I had was a napkin.

She was getting worse. I hadn't bothered to confront her over the pretending to be in Lockie's bed incident. It didn't feel important enough to argue about since it had no basis in reality.

"You and Counterpoint are a novice team," Lockie said. "But if you don't want to go to Florida, that's fine with me."

"Would you like some more coffee?" Jules asked him.

"I'd better not," he said.

We weren't sure that coffee wasn't partially the cause of his headaches and had decided to limit him to one cup a day. So far so good.

Greer shrieked at us and stomped into the house.

Jules began clearing the table as my father stood to leave.

"I'll call the school and tell them you won't be attending this year," he said.

"Thank you, Dad."

Lockie finished his eggs and placed his fork on the plate. "So what's going on?"

"I want to stay home."

"Why?"

He waited while I tried to find the right words.

"You know how you said getting on the pony that first time made you know where you belonged?"

Lockie nodded.

"I know where I belong now."

He stood. "Then let's get the day going."

***

I was still setting up fences in the indoor when Greer arrived on Counterpoint.

"Where's Lockie?"

"He's on the phone. Someone is interested in buying Sans."

Greer shrugged at the thought her former equitation horse would be moving to a new home. "He's a good horse for someone with no aspirations."

My half-sister was delusional most of the time. She was like the people who lined up for the American Idol auditions and hadn't prepared for the performance. As a policy, Greer thought that the work leading up to the event was, if not beneath her, at least uninteresting.

I put the last pole up on the jump standard. "Why are you putting us through this?"

"What are you talking about?"

"You ride Counterpoint half as often as you should. You said you wanted to make it to the National Horse Show then didn't practice . . ."

"Nicole Boisvert!" Greer shouted.

As if that explained everything.

"Yes, Nicole is the top junior ride in the country but that doesn't mean . . ." I started.

"She is unbeatable."

"Okay, you couldn't beat her. Now what's your excuse?

You can't blame Counterpoint because he's fantastic. When I see Derry ride him . . . "

"You think he's so much better than I am?"

"Greer. Derry is a better rider than you are."

We had hired Derry to exercise Counterpoint because Greer couldn't be counted upon to maintain a schedule. He was very capable and far more reliable about showing up than she was.

Sometimes people needed to be told the truth. It was a disservice to mislead them and Greer had been pampered for too long.

"Why do you have to be so hateful?" Greer asked softly.

I was shocked. She'd never used that tone of voice in my presence before.

"I don't hate you and I'm not trying to hurt you. On the contrary, I'm trying to help you."

"How is that a help?"

"You should deal with reality."

"That everyone is a better rider than I am?"

"That's not true. You have all the potential in the world but you don't apply yourself," I replied.

"That's the kind of bull your mother shoveled at you."

"Excuse me?"

"If you work hard you'll succeed. If you're good, good things will happen to you. It doesn't always work."

I sighed. "Nothing always works. In real life, most things

don't work. Most of the time you fail. Sometimes you fail when you should succeed."

"Then why try?" Greer asked.

"When did you ever fail?"

"It's none of your damn business."

The old Greer was back.

"Okay. You have a great horse and a great trainer. It's up to you to write your future."

"Bullshit, bullshit, bullshit," Greer said as she rode to the far end of the arena.

Lockie entered by the side door and walked over to me.

"I'm sorry. I made things worse with her."

"You don't have to apologize. She's Lady Weathervane independent of you."

I nodded.

"Come on, people, this isn't the only thing I have to do today," Greer called.

"I don't know why she says things like that. It is the only thing she has to do today," I said.

"Because she doesn't like to be judged and found lacking either," Lockie replied.

I paused. "I'd like to spend some time with you."

"Do you want to go for a hack after dinner?"

I smiled. "Is that like a date?"

"Yes, like a date."

* * *

We rode up into the hills, didn't talk much and it was the perfect way to end the day. As we rode back into the stable yard it was getting dark and a car came down the driveway with its lights on. It stopped and the door opened.

"Hi."

"Hi, Josh," I said throwing a leg over CB's neck and sliding to the ground.

"I thought I could talk to you for a while."

"Sure."

"Hi, Lockie. I'm sorry if I seemed rude. I wasn't ignoring you," Josh said.

"No, Josh, I'm sure you were just excited to see her. A lot of people feel that way about Talia but so often not in a good way."

"Lockie!"

He held out his hand and motioned to the reins I was holding.

"I'll take care of CB, you have a visit with Josh."

"But . . ."

"I'll come up to the house when I'm done."

I paused.

"Go," Lockie said.

"Maybe I should have called first, it seems like you two were . . ."

"You're welcome here any time, Josh," Lockie said. "Go have some cookies and milk and I'll get there when the horses are turned out."

* * *

I poured some ginger ale for Josh knowing he preferred that to cola when he had a choice and brought out a platter of chocolate-orange biscotti Jules had made earlier in the week. Josh sat at the table on the terrace, in his favorite chair, at least it was the one he wound up using if I wasn't already in it.

Josh was my oldest friend, besides Rogers, and I didn't want to grow so far apart we never saw each other anymore. I expected we would go in different directions after graduation but had never pictured what that would be like in practice.

"Rogers called me this afternoon. She was unhappy," Josh said.

I had told her of my change of plans. "About my leaving The Briar School?"

"Yes. Why are you doing it?"

"I can see my future," I replied.

"Are you getting agoraphobic?"

I laughed. "No, I'm not afraid to leave the farm. I don't want to leave. I have other things to do. You know how that is. You went off on the grand tour across the country. You were following your dream."

"What kind of dream is it to stay here?" Josh asked as he broke a biscotti in two and took a bite.

"I wouldn't characterize it in quite the same way but it's

like anything you're called to do. You want to get on with it instead of wasting time."

"It's only a year. You'll graduate next spring."

"A year is a long time."

"Don't think of it in terms of your mother," he told me.

I bit into a cookie and chewed for a moment. "You don't know what life holds for you. Your days are always numbered."

"Talia, you can't be preoccupied by this."

"That's what everyone says but I think they're wrong. If you are always aware of how precious each moment is, then when you reach that last one, you won't feel a sense of lost opportunity."

Josh regarded me evenly. "You're sure?"

"It's only high school. I still have to study. My father is getting me a tutor. You will just have to eat lunch with Rogers every day instead having a fine dining experience with me."

"I can't talk you out of it?"

I finished my biscotti. "Not anymore than I could have talked you out of going on the road this summer."

"Is it because of Lockie?" Josh asked.

"Partially, yes."

"You're engaged or something?"

"The 'or something' part is close."

"We were good friends," Josh said. "I want you to be happy."

"Are good friends. Nothing's changed. I want you to be happy, too."

From the dark, Lockie stepped up onto the terrace. "Is it a private conversation? Do you need more time?"

"No," Josh said. "I was waiting for you."

Lockie sat in his usual seat.

"Have a biscotti. Would you like tea or milk?" I pushed the plate closer to him.

"What are you having?" Lockie asked me.

"We had ginger ale."

"May I have milk?"

"Of course." I got up and went into the kitchen. A moment later, I put the glass in front of him.

"Thank you."

There was silence but for the sound of frogs down at the pond.

"Paxton is coming up from the city for a few days and I hoped you would join us for dinner at the Garnet Inn," Josh said.

I glanced over to Lockie to see what his reaction would be. We hadn't been out to dinner or anything like a date and didn't want him pressured into something he wasn't ready for. He might have joked that our hack was a date but it more closely resembled being in the same place at the same time.

"I would like you to get to know him," Josh said.

"Have you told your parents," I asked before Lockie could frame the words.

"No."

"How are you explaining this visit?"

"That he's a friend from summer stock."

"And Paxton has no objection to this . . . ruse?"

"It's not the easiest thing in the world to come out to your parents, especially when they're like mine," Josh admitted.

I didn't envy him this confrontation, for it was bound to be unpleasant. It was no surprise that he was reluctant to spring it on them, and was delaying the scene for as long as possible.

"Why is Paxton coming for a visit if you can't be honest?" I asked.

"He wants to get out of the city and my parents have a very large house. It's not as though we never have guests."

That was true. The Standishes loved company, enjoyed being surrounded by people and were always ready to entertain on major and minor holidays. The first Halloween party I attended at their estate was like Disney World on hallucinogens with princesses and zombies dancing together while enormous glowing pumpkin sky lanterns were freed to rise into the darkness overhead.

"It's fine. We'll go to dinner and meet Paxton," Lockie said.

Josh stood. "Good. I'll call you when the specifics are set," he said then hesitated.

I waited for him to say something else.

"Yeah. Have a good night," Josh added uncomfortably then went down the path to the driveway.

Lockie and I sat in the near dark for a while without speaking. Periodically, I could hear one of the horses.

"I'm surprised you agreed to going out to dinner," I said.

"Why?"

"We've never been out."

"Do you want to go somewhere?"

Where he was, was where I wanted to be. "This is good."

"Something isn't right with Josh."

"Do you mean why would he ask us to have dinner with them when he could be alone with Paxton? I'm just his beard again. He's putting on a show for his parents, to make it seem casual when his friend comes up from the city."

"Is that what it is?" Lockie stood. "I want you to put CB into training for the hunter pace."

"What does that mean?"

"You both need to work on your endurance. Twenty minutes a day and a hack isn't putting either of you in shape. We need to increase your fitness level."

"Rogers, too?"

"Yes."

I knew there was more to it than that. "You're thinking."

"I won't ask you to do anything you can't do."

"How about extending that to anything I don't want to do?"

Lockie laughed.

That meant no.

IT WAS AFTER MIDNIGHT when there was a knock on my door. Before I could respond, Greer came in. She looked as though she had had a hard night.

"Why are you leaving me alone at school?"

This was someone who rarely greeted me if we passed in the hall and had never eaten lunch with me except at home. I had never been admitted into her social circle.

"Excuse me?"

"Freaking hell! I'm supposed to go there alone?"

"All your friends are there."

She kicked my boots out of her way as she strode across the room. "Are you staying home to be with Lockie?"

"No, I'm staying home to be with Dad."

"Liar!"

"Why ask if you know you won't believe me?"

"Why would you stay home to be with him when he's not here?"

"He's going to change his schedule around for a few months."

"He was my father first!"

Greer was so agitated, I almost thought she was going to start ripping her clothes to shreds.

"For a couple months, that's true."

A few months older than I was, that was a fact Greer never let me forget, although I wasn't sure why it was important.

"He lived with us!"

It was hardly necessary to point that out as I had spent most of my life trying to get past that sense of abandonment. "You had your time with him and now I'm going to have my time with him."

"I don't want you to be with him! I hate this!"

I didn't know what to say, knowing everything Greer said was true. What was hers was out of bounds to anyone else. It was something of a surprise she let Derry ride Counterpoint, but she would never let him use her saddle.

It was a shock that she felt so proprietary of our father since what she usually did was shriek at him.

"Are you doing this to me because of Lockie?"

"Greer, get a grip. I'm not doing anything to you. I don't live my life in reaction to you."

Dressed in sweats, hair mussed, Jules entered the room. "What's going on?"

"Nothing!"

"You're scaring the horses." Jules gave me a sidelong glance and I started to laugh. This was an old joke between us and even though it applied to the new-fangled automobiles scaring carriage horses a hundred years ago, it always seemed to fit Greer like a pair of custom-made boots.

"Come downstairs with me, Greer, and I'll make you a cup of tea."

"I don't want any tea! I want my childhood back!"

I'm sure my mouth dropped open at that, since I didn't realize she was capable of that level of reflection. Maybe it was only because she was drunk or high or whatever it was.

Before anything else could be said, my father entered the room, took Greer by the arm and dragged her out into the hallway. There was scuffling all the way back to her room where the door opened and closed with a bang.

Jules came over and sat on the edge of my bed. "Are you okay?"

"Yes, I'm fine."

I had become inured to her tantrums by this point.

"I'm sorry she's so high-strung."

I closed the book I was reading and turned off my reader. "That's a nice way to put it."

Jules stood. "Are you going to be able to get to sleep?"

"Not for a long time."

"Would you like some chamomile tea?"

"No, thanks."

"I'll go make some for Greer. The gesture counts for something."

I nodded and Jules left the room.

Getting out of bed, I pulled on my jeans and a sweatshirt. Somewhere in the dark, there was a horse with a warm neck I could put my arms around.

* * *

Finding CB in the field, I led him to the fence and got on, just lying down on his back as he went back to grazing. I don't know how long I stayed there. It was until Greer's temper tantrum had dissolved into the night sky and until I started to feel a little sleepy. Then I slid off and left him to his pals.

As I was crossing through the stable yard, I saw a shadow in the open doorway.

"You startled me!"

"What were you doing?"

"Visiting CB. Greer threw a temper tantrum and I needed to be close to him."

"Why didn't you come to me?" Lockie asked as he turned then closed the door and I was left in the darkness.

I slept fitfully, woke early and was already taking milk out of the refrigerator when Jules entered the kitchen.

"Why didn't you sleep late after last night?"

"Because I was just laying there thinking too much. It was better to get the day going."

"Try not to let Greer bother you."

"Easier said than done. Teach me how to make breakfast."

"Okay. What would you like?"

"Let's start with something easy."

Jules thought for a moment. "We have some croissants left over. Let's make a caramel pecan sauce, layer the croissants in that and put that in the oven for about twenty minutes. While that's baking, we'll make omelets. How does that sound?"

"Wonderful."

She made the caramel sauce, while I stood to the side trying not to be burned by the molten sugar. We cut the croissants in half and after the sauce was in the baking dish, I arranged the slices in as neatly as possible.

By the time breakfast was prepared, it was raining. Lockie didn't arrive. My father was in his office conducting business and Greer was upstairs sleeping it off. Jules and I ate together in the kitchen while she told me how hard it had been to leave home and go to cooking school in France. She had done exactly the opposite of me but for the same reason. Jules thought she would find herself in France and I thought I would find my place at home.

After packing breakfast for Lockie, I drove to the barn. It was raining harder than an hour ago and I found him in a long waxed raincoat and rubber wellington boots coming in from the field. His expression was as dark as the sky.

"What's wrong? Is it about last night?"

"It's about last night but nothing to do with you. Keynote ran into something and has a puncture wound on his stifle. The vet's on his way."

"Is it bad?"

"Yes, it's deep. It'll heal but it'll leave a scar. I was out there trying to find what it was."

"The fields are so clean."

"They are." He walked past me, running his hand over his wet hair.

"I brought breakfast for you."

Lockie turned to look at me. "So what's the answer from last night?"

"I didn't choose CB over you, I chose him instead of you."

He nodded. "Maybe you should spend the morning up at the house."

"Lockie. You're that upset with me?"

"Yeah."

"Can't we talk about this?"

I heard a truck drive in and Lockie looked down the aisle to the stable yard.

"That's the vet."

There was no time and no sense in trying to continue

the discussion. I placed the market basket on top of a bale of hay. "Okay."

Exiting the barn, I got in my truck and drove back to the house.

* * *

I tapped on the library door.

"Come in." He looked up from his papers. "Talia."

"Do you have a minute?"

"Just about that. I have a conference call in a few minutes. I can be here but can't take off."

"I understand," I replied sitting in my chair.

"Has Greer always treated you the way she did last night?" he said.

"Pretty much."

"I'm sorry. I should have noticed."

"No, she's good at covering up. I know you're busy so I'll get right to this. The apartment over the barn hasn't been upgraded for as long as I've lived here. The furniture is worn out. It would be nice to paint and get some new pieces before winter. I thought we could find someone to take care of that."

The phone began ringing and my father reached for it.

"No."

I was zero for two.

* * *

As part of my acquisition of life skills, I watched Jules make soup for lunch.

"Why aren't you at the barn?"

"We had a misunderstanding and I got booted out."

Jules continued to dice mushrooms. "That sounds like more than a misunderstanding."

"No, that's all."

Greer, barefooted and in an oversize tee-shirt, practically staggered into the kitchen. "What time is it?"

"Time for you to take a shower and get dressed," Jules replied.

"Eleven," I told her.

"Where's the aspirin?" Greer asked as she turned.

"In the bathroom."

"Not mine."

"Take mine," I said.

Greer bumped into the doorway and left.

"What are you going to do about the misunderstanding," Jules asked.

"Turn it into an understanding," I replied, standing up.

Taking my raincoat off the rack by the door, I went outside and to my truck. On the short trip to the barn, I still didn't have a clue what to say to him. I wished it was possible to say nothing, but it wasn't.

Tracy was on the aisle grooming Counterpoint and she glanced up as I hurried inside. I could see Wingspread wasn't in his stall.

"If you're looking for Lockie, he's in the indoor," she told me, clippers in hand.

"Thanks."

It was raining harder than before and when I reached the doorway, Lockie and Wing had just turned off the track and were angling across the arena performing a half pass at a canter.

The move was performed to perfection and I realized how much he had to miss competing. For Lockie, riding and training was only half the equation. It was enough for me but for him so much was missing. To live with that aspect of his ability unused and unresolved had to be endlessly frustrating.

He pulled Wing to a halt next to me, didn't say anything and didn't smile.

I looked up at him. "I know you don't want to discuss what happened last night so I'll keep it brief. For years, I had no one here but Butch. If I can't make the transition to relying on a human over the course of a summer, maybe that's not so incomprehensible. As for why I chose CB instead of you, that was simple. It was midnight and I thought you needed to sleep. Just because I can't sleep doesn't mean you have to put your health at risk."

"I don't want you to be my nursemaid," Lockie replied.

"Is that how you feel?"

"Sometimes, yes."

Maybe it was a habit of mine.

Lockie dismounted. "You want to take care of me."

"I do."

"Did it ever occur to you that I might want to take care of you?"

"No."

It hadn't.

"That's the problem." Lockie turned and began running up his stirrup irons. "Unless you have no interest in that. Maybe you just want me to be Butch. Keep me in the barn and double-wrap me so I don't bump myself."

Sometimes there is no right thing to say. Emotions have a logic of their own and can move on undercurrents that eddy, surface and submerge.

"That's true. I don't want you to bump yourself."

"I'm just an echo of your mother."

"That's not true."

"Yes, it is. You're reliving your fear of loss through me. You keep a distance between us so you won't be hurt again. That's why Josh was so safe for you. You loved that relationship because it was going nowhere. Out of misplaced kindness, you're still enabling Josh to perpetuate the pretense that he's a straight guy."

"If I was trying to maintain a distance from you so I wouldn't get hurt, it didn't work," I replied.

I had thought it would be easier than this. Apologize, have lunch, ride the horses in the afternoon.

"How long is it going to take you to get past this?"

Lockie pulled the reins over Wingspread's head. "This is reality."

"Okay. Rogers is coming for a lesson this afternoon, should I come down to help you or not?"

"No."

"Then I'll tell Greer she can have you."

"Yeah, do that."

* * *

I left the indoor, climbed in my truck and drove to the tack shop where I splurged on halter nameplates for CB and Wing, gloves for me, fox earrings for Greer, a cute scarf for Jules, and a polo shirt in our stable color, bittersweet red, for Lockie. At the farm market, I bought a fifty-pound bag of carrots for the horses and a human size bag of what were close to the last of the peaches for my father.

I wanted to call Rogers so we could meet at the diner for a cup of tea and gossip but she was at the barn having a lesson. Instead of going down there to ride CB, it seemed smarter to simply take the day off. It was still pouring and I decided to declutter my bedroom. There were clothes for school I wouldn't be wearing anymore so packing them up and leaving them at the local church to distribute to whoever might need them made sense. Books, too, would be packed up then donated to the library for their periodic sales.

Leaving the fruit on the counter, I went upstairs and

spent the next hours putting my past into boxes, resisting all notions of saving just this one thing. Whatever it was, someone else needed it more than I did.

The rain hadn't stopped by the time I went downstairs to the kitchen.

"It's just us," Jules said.

"Where's Dad?"

"He left while you were out and asked me to tell you he'll be staying overnight in the city so he can catch an early flight to St. Louis tomorrow."

"That's not unexpected, is it?"

"No," Jules admitted.

"And Lockie?"

"Called and said he was passing on dinner."

I sighed. Lockie missed lunch and wouldn't have dinner unless he scavenged something at his apartment but he'd made it quite clear I wasn't supposed to function as his nursemaid.

I never saw it that way but if he did, that was the reality. Lockie was a big enough boy to take care of himself. Even if I didn't quite believe it.

Jules and I had dinner together at the kitchen table and afterward she brought dessert of roasted peaches and custard sauce. I heated water for tea and we sat there for about an hour talking about her extended family whom she missed terribly and I would finally get to meet in a few months.

We cleaned up the kitchen then I went back to my room, got into bed and read until I felt sleepy. I was trying to be philosophical about my life. The farther along I went, the less control I seemed to have over important events. It was easy to get a new pair of jeans or even to quit going to The Briar School but in big matters such as my mother's health, Lockie's well-being, finding the key to Greer's discontent, it was all impossible. Even my father, who was so accustomed to giving orders and making things happen, couldn't change what was meant to be.

I felt somehow comforted that I was just going along for the ride. It took so much pressure off me to imagine that I might only be responsible for myself and how I chose to react. That was all of it. As I slid into sleep, I remembered my mother had told me this many times but it was something I had forgotten.

My phone on the nightstand rang, waking me up. It was absolutely dark, deep into the middle of the night.

"Talia. Could you come down here?"

"I'll be right there."

— 5 —

I RAN UP THE STAIRS and knocked on his door. "Lockie."

There was no answer.

I tried the knob. It turned so I let myself in. I didn't see him on the floor, which was what I expected. "Lockie!"

"I'm in the bathroom."

A moment later, the door opened and he came into the room unsteadily.

"Do you need to go to the hospital?"

He was pale enough to look like the answer was yes.

"No."

"Are you sure?"

"Yes." He walked to the sofa and sat down slowly, as if it took everything he had just to do that.

I pulled off my raincoat and dropped it over one of the wooden chairs. "What's going on?"

"I've been throwing up all day."

"When's the last time you ate?"

"Breakfast."

"So nothing is coming up anymore."

"No."

"Have you been drinking water?"

"I tried but that came back up, too."

I sat down beside him and pinched the skin on his hand then let it go. When it didn't snap right back I knew he was dehydrated.

"What would you do for Butch?" Lockie asked.

"Make him a warm mash with diced apples."

"Since I'm not eating wet bran . . . it looks like you're my nursemaid anyway."

"I may be a lot of things to you, but that's not one of them. Let's just put that aside and deal with the problem at hand."

"What else would you do for Butch?"

"Stay with him and hold his hoof."

"Hold my hoof."

I took his hand. "We need to replace some of those fluids you've been losing."

"No thanks. Throwing up isn't that much fun."

"Let's try. Do you have some of the coconut water I got

for you?" I had a standing order at an online site to send a case every week.

He pointed to about three cases stacked by the kitchenette.

"You're supposed to be drinking them."

"I forget."

I stood. "Okay. That's good in a way, at least we have plenty now. So we'll both have one, we'll sip together."

"Tali, there's no point."

Cutting open the box with a knife laying on the counter, I pulled out two containers. There were clean glasses in the dishwasher so I brought those to the coffee table.

"When then?"

"In the morning?"

"No, because I'll be driving you to the hospital by then, so they can put you on an IV."

"I don't want to go to the hospital."

I handed him a glass of coconut water. "Drink."

Lockie regarded the liquid doubtfully but put the glass to his lips and sipped. "I'm sorry about earlier."

"You were more right than wrong, so I thank for that."

"You thank me?"

"Sometimes people need to hear the truth. It can be a kindness."

"Sometimes I wind up saying things I shouldn't." He sipped again.

"We all do. How do you feel?"

"Besides that it feels like a truck ran over my head, so far so good."

We sat in silence for a while, the rain drumming on the roof.

"Does this remind you of your mother?"

"A little bit," I admitted.

"I'm sorry."

"There's nothing to be sorry about. I was glad to be able to help her and I'm glad to be able to help you. It's a privilege."

Lockie sipped his juice.

"When you were sick as a child, what did your mother make you to eat?"

He looked at me and shrugged.

"She must had made you some treat."

"I guess I was never sick enough to stay home from school."

"Ever?"

"I don't remember it."

"You don't remember or you don't remember it happening?"

"Most of my long-term memory is still intact. It depends on what the definition is of long-term. For some people, there's a clear demarcation between the past and the accident. For others, the edge is blurred."

"Like meeting Alise at the Standish party."

"I did not recognize her. Maybe I met her that week.

Maybe I met her at the event grounds. I'm told we were there for three days."

"That must be very difficult."

Lockie smiled. "It's not."

He had almost finished his glass of coconut water.

"Do you feel any better now?"

"Yes. Would you stay here tonight and keep me company?"

"Of course." I would never have left him there alone anyway. The nursemaid in me knew that was not a wise plan. Either I was staying there or he was coming back to the house.

I couldn't risk the chance that Lockie might become dizzy on the way to the bathroom. That had happened to my mother often enough and at least she had me in the apartment with her.

"I have a question." He tipped the glass up and drained what was left of the liquid. "You treat me like Butch."

I popped the top of another can and poured it into his glass. "Are we going there again?"

"Yes."

"What, then? Yes, you asked me to treat you like I treat Butch and I do."

"You don't, though. I see you put your arms around Butch. I see you kiss him. I see you kiss CB. But you don't kiss me. Why not?"

I didn't reply.

"Is it because of your father? Because I work for him? Because of Greer and Rui? You once said that the only thing that would get me fired was if I had sex with Greer. Is that the reason you keep your distance or is it something else?"

"Should I take this opportunity to point out that you've never kissed me?"

"I didn't think you wanted me to."

"I did, okay?"

"Did you ever think of mentioning that or acting upon it?"

"Yes, I considered it and decided being like Greer was not a good idea."

"Who's going to mistake you for Greer? Greer can't keep her clothes on."

"The first day you were here, you laughed over Greer's reputation. I didn't know if you thought I was like her." I finished my water. "She walks that walk."

"Professional escorts could take lessons from her."

It hurt me to hear that about my half-sister but it was true. "And she doesn't wear a bra."

"Luckily there's not that much there to bounce."

"Lockie!"

"That's a good way to make sure I don't ask for a sitting trot."

Poor Greer. So desperate for attention. She was fortunate Lockie didn't take advantage of her lack of common sense. I wondered if she was aware of that.

"Do you want to go up to the house and I'll make you some chicken soup with noodles? Jules always has stock in the freezer. It'll just take a couple minutes."

"No, thank you, I'm very happily not sick to my stomach right now and don't change the subject."

"You shouldn't take it personally that I keep my distance from everyone. Yes, we can say Josh used me as his beard but I used him, too. As long as we were considered a couple, no one would annoy us with questions or expectations. They didn't wonder if he was gay . . ."

"How was that enough for you? For Josh, I get it because I'm sure he was conducting business on the side."

I looked at him in surprise. "You're sure?"

"You didn't know?"

"No."

Lockie nodded. "Yes, I'm sure."

"It was enough for me. I had Butch, and Rogers and Josh as a friend. I knew that someday I'd move away and . . ."

"But you're doing just the opposite. You're staying home."

I shrugged. "The situation isn't the same anymore."

Lockie made everything different.

He put the glass down on what passed for a coffee table. "Do you think you can sleep next to me?"

I shrugged. "I don't sleep very well."

"You'll hold my hand and by first light . . ."

"What?"

Lockie stood. "We'll wake up and I'll look at your beautiful face in confusion and say 'Who are you?'"

He pulled me to my feet and kissed my temple. "This is so exciting, Silly Filly. Our first night together!"

There was no bedroom in the apartment, just a corner of the space where the bed was. We lay down on top of the covers, he took my hand, we listened to the rain on the roof and I fell asleep.

* * *

He woke me by kissing my cheek. "We have to get the day going, Silly."

"What time is it?"

"Six. The horses need to be fed and in fifteen minutes Jules is going to wonder where you are."

"How do you feel?"

"It's like a hangover, something you know nothing about I'm sure. I still have a headache, but it's an improvement over yesterday. Once I take the meds, it'll be better so don't worry about me."

"Can you eat some breakfast?"

"Some."

"How about a bowl of cream of wheat?"

He was going through the clothes basket looking for a clean shirt. "What?"

"You've never had it?"

"No."

"It's a hot cereal."

"Like we eat hot cereal in California."

"My mother used to make it for me and it would be good for you. It's bland. I think there are some raspberries in the refrigerator."

Lockie pulled off the shirt he had slept in and pulled the fresh one on. "Is it like a bran mash?"

"It's white."

"So white bran mash."

"Without the bran."

He made a face. "Why don't you go up to the house first? You could say you got up early to feed the horses before anyone else was awake."

I stood, finger-combed my hair and crossed to the door. "You don't have to cover for me. I think we're past that, aren't we?"

"I would prefer it."

"Then that's what it is."

We fed, watered, and threw the horses hay, then climbed in my truck and drove to the house. My father was in Missouri so I didn't have to face him but Jules would require an explanation. If we got lucky, Greer would be asleep until we started working in the indoor.

As we entered the kitchen from the terrace, Jules looked up from the melon that she was cutting into chunks. "I know it's not any of my business but is there anything I should know? Something I should keep quiet about?"

"Absolutely not. I wouldn't want you lying for me to begin with," I said pulling off my raincoat.

Lockie followed me into the house. "I didn't feel well yesterday."

"Is that why you didn't eat?"

"Yes. I asked Tali to come down to the apartment and keep me company for a while."

I found the box of cereal in the cabinet. "Would you make him some cream of wheat? Do we still have some raspberries?"

"A pint."

"I'll make the tea."

"Why can't I have a hamburger?" Lockie asked.

"You can for lunch," Jules said. "I'll make some brioche rolls. Is noon a good time?"

"I'm hungry now."

"You can have some toast," she replied.

"You two are ganging up on me," Lockie said.

Jules and I nodded.

* * *

By midmorning, I was on CB doing a kindergarten level dressage test in the indoor. I turned CB down the ring's centerline and halted as squarely as possible.

"What you do is perform all the required elements but still as if you are riding hunter seat."

"I don't understand."

"You're a wonderful equitation rider."

"Am not."

"Yes, you are, but that's in your past."

"If I was so wonderful at it," I said over him, "why didn't I place over Greer ever? All I ever was, was passable. Please don't try to make me feel adequate."

"You're right. I won't try to make you feel adequate." Lockie shook his head and turned away then turned back. "You didn't want to place over Greer."

"Excuse me?"

"You've been doing just enough to appear competent."

"How do you figure that?"

"A good rider gets a lot out of a horse without taking a lot out of him. You did remarkable work on Butch, who is, frankly, not very talented. CB adores you. He would do anything for you."

"He would do anything for you," I replied.

"With persuasion. For you, he does everything with enthusiasm. That's where the swish comes from, but I wish he'd knock that move off."

"How do you know this?"

"I can see it by watching the two of you go around the ring. Get off."

"What?"

Lockie came over to us and I slid to the ground. In one effortless move, Lockie was in the saddle and turned CB to the track.

"This is how you canter."

He put CB into a canter. It looked fine to me.

"This is a working canter."

A moment later, there was a subtle but discernible change in the way CB was moving. He seemed more in balance, more compressed, the gait was rounded and his weight slightly to his hindquarters.

"Think tempo. Think light. Three separate, deliberate beats."

There was nothing hurried about the canter as CB and Lockie went around the arena and it was as different as night from day compared to what I was accustomed to.

Lockie pulled CB to a walk and turned toward me.

"CB must be very talented," I said.

"Very."

"He's patient with me, isn't he?"

Lockie smiled. "Yes, he's happy."

"Why should he be so pleased?"

Lockie slid off. "Because you're a kind person and a gentle rider."

I reached out, took Lockie's shirt, pulled him to me and kissed his cheek.

"That is so much better. Now you're treating me like Butch."

Lockie kissed me in return.

It was so much better.

"Am I interrupting something?" Greer asked coming through the doorway.

"Yes."

"No."

She looked at me then Lockie. "I didn't want you anyway."

"You already have Derry," I remarked.

"Yeah. Are we still having a lesson today or are you two going to make out in the hay loft until lunch?"

"That's a good suggestion but no," Lockie replied as he gave me a leg up onto CB. "Tack Counterpoint and warm him up. Talia will be done in ten minutes."

Greer turned and headed for the door then turned back. "Are you two . . ."

I waited.

"You are." She shrugged. "What do you think Dad will say?"

"Good choice." Lockie replied.

"Do I still have that schooling show in two weeks?"

"Yes."

"Will I be ready for it?"

"If you start working now, yes," Lockie said.

Greer nodded and left the indoor.

"Will she be ready?"

"Yes. What does she have to do but stay on and steer?"

"Is Counterpoint that good?"

"Yes. He's worth every penny your father spent."

"If you rode him, would he be successful at the national level?"

"Yes. Why?"

"Would you be happier if you rode him?"

"No. Open jumping is not my thing. Wing agrees so we're very compatible."

"Why isn't it Wing's thing?"

"He can jump four feet very reliably but not five. Counterpoint can easily do the five."

"Why can't you turn Counterpoint into an event horse?"

"I don't think he has the temperament for it. He's like Greer and doesn't want to be bothered with details. For both of them, it's step on the gas and go."

"And CB is the opposite."

"Polar opposite."

"And Wing is?"

"Perfect. Right in the middle. CB, this is not a criticism of him, is too calm. He doesn't have the speed or attitude needed for cross-country. A hundred years ago, he would have been fine. The competition has gotten sharper and faster. He's an excellent dressage horse and we didn't get him for speed, we got him for your comfort."

I nodded.

"Why are we talking when you're supposed to be working?"

"I want to know you," I replied.

"Know me at lunch. Canter and see if you can get him balanced this time."

Inside leg at the girth, outside leg slightly behind the girth, and CB began cantering.

"Hold him together. Stabilize him. Use your back."

I felt the change.

"There you go."

"It's a different place in the saddle," I said.

"Yes."

Greer entered the ring on Counterpoint. "Do you have time for me?"

"I'll try to squeeze you in," Lockie replied.

I leaned over in the saddle to be closer to him. "I'll be right back to help you with the fences. Try to . . . make her feel good about herself."

"How, in the name of all that's rational, is that possible?" Lockie asked softly.

"Try."

I rode out of the arena, slid off CB, kissed his muzzle and brought him into the barn. As I untacked him, I told him how much I enjoyed our time together and what a good companion he was. His ears followed me as I worked around him and gave his tail a tug. "You're quite the charmer."

I returned CB to his stall, made sure he had some hay, gave him a hug and told him he'd have lunch as soon as I got back. When I slid the door shut, I turned and saw CB trying to push his nose between the bars. It occurred to me that if the bars were removed on the door, everyone could put their heads out and see what was going on but still not reach their neighbor with unwanted attention.

When I returned to the indoor, Greer was just finishing her work on the flat. As I watched her canter around the ring, I could only appreciate Greer's technique and position. It might not have appeared that she was paying attention during lessons, but obviously she had been. Greer was such a good rider, I wished that her focus over the past months had been more on perfecting her equestrian skills than on enhancing her social life. It made me wonder why that was so. She wasn't stupid. She had to know that taking so much time away from the barn would hurt her chances to qualify for the Maclay more than help.

For the next twenty minutes, I helped Lockie set up fences, changing the height and spread. There was an oxer, an in and out, a panel and verticals but show jumping wasn't only about the size of the fences, it was about speed, tight turns and taking obstacles at an angle in order to save time.

Since Greer was going to a schooling show, the tests wouldn't be very strenuous but a lesson with Lockie wasn't a stroll down the lane. He was pushing her and Counterpoint hard but Greer didn't have the kind of personality that would cause her to back down. There was a stubborn streak in her a mile wide and two miles deep.

When Lockie finally ended the lesson, Greer was exhausted and Counterpoint was wet. I followed her into the barn where I helped take care of Counterpoint and Lockie went up to his apartment to clean up for lunch.

"You did a nice job today," I told her while hosing him down and Greer used the sweat scrapper.

"If that's true, why do I have to go to a schooling show?"

"Everyone goes to schooling shows, it's not beneath you."

"Cam Rafferty doesn't go to schooling shows."

Of course she had to pick one of the top riders in the country.

"Stay home for a change, ride, practice, don't fight Lockie over every damn thing he asks you to do, and maybe in a year you'll be one of the top riders in the country and you can have a peon take your horses to schooling shows."

"You're such a bitch!"

"You're . . ."

"What am I?"

"Mistaken if you think this success you seek will be handed to you just because you're the prettiest girl on the show circuit."

Greer dropped the sweat scraper on the floor of the wash stall and left the barn.

I picked up the scraper and finished the job as Lockie entered.

"What's with her now?"

What was the point in trying to explain Greer who, emotionally, could be like someone on ice skates for the first time. "Can we take the day off?"

Lockie paused. "Okay. Why?"

"Let's go somewhere."

"Where?"

I thought. "The Harriet Beecher Stowe Museum."

He looked at me in confusion.

"It doesn't matter where. Inside because it's raining. Some place quiet. Any place Greer won't be."

Lockie put his arm around me and pulled me to him. "Greer's not actually that unusual. The horse show circuit is full of girls just like her. Wealthy, and spoiled, she thinks she should have whatever she wants when she wants it and when she doesn't get it she becomes a three-year old at the supermarket."

"You mean Greer needs a nap?"

"It wouldn't hurt."

"You could be describing me," I replied.

Lockie kissed my cheek. "No, I could not be."

My phone began ringing.

"Get it," Lockie said as he unclipped Counterpoint and walked him back to his stall.

I pulled the phone out of my back pocket and clicked it on. Josh. "Hi."

"Hi. How are you? Moldy yet?"

"Close to it."

"I know this is short notice but are you free for dinner tonight? Paxton came up and tomorrow we're going to New Haven to see a play. I'd invite you but it's not something you'd want to see."

"Something like *Boys Under the Bus?*"

"*Boys in the Band*, yes, something like that."

A couple weeks ago Josh had been in a summer stock performance of a play so boring, Lockie and I left after the first act. I couldn't imagine what he would see with his new boyfriend. It wasn't going to be *Camelot* unless it was an all-male cast and everyone had a thing for Lancelot.

"Have fun," I replied.

"So is it yes?" Josh asked.

Lockie closed Counterpoint's stall door. I just wanted to spend some time with him alone.

"Yes," I told Josh. "Text me the directions and time. See you."

"Thanks, Tali."

I clicked off.

"Who was that?"

"Josh. We're having dinner with him and the boyfriend tonight. Is that okay with you?"

"Sure."

"You can't accuse me of being his beard anymore."

"Let's go have lunch," Lockie said and took my hand.

6

WE DIDN'T GO ANYWHERE SPECIAL that afternoon because some customers called and wanted to look at Blue Moon, a small roan mare Lockie had picked up to sell a few weeks back. He was intent on paying my father back for Wingspread and the hospital bill resulting from his accident. Flipping horses, buying to sell quickly, was one way. There wasn't a huge investment in time or training. The process relied on Lockie's ability to find talented prospects and match them up with the right customer.

Lockie needn't feel so pressured by the financial situation and it concerned me how hard he worked and the long hours he put in. It hadn't been a loan, and my father was well-known for his generosity but I thought he admired Lockie for his determination to owe nothing.

Putting Blue Moon through the standard equitation requirements in the indoor while Lockie spoke to the family, when their thirteen year old daughter got on, I went back to the house, disappointed that we hadn't spent time together as I had hoped.

Feeling as though there was something missing in my life, I didn't know what it was. I tried to convince myself it was just the disruption of splitting with Josh, while at the same time I was leaving school in my senior year. Changes in routine can be difficult and that's all I wanted this to be.

As I sat in my bedroom chair, trying to remain focused on the book in my lap and failing miserably because all I kept thinking about was how much I would like to tell my mother everything that had been happening this summer, how much my life had shifted again like a tectonic plate in an earthquake. It was the same as it always had been but inhabited another place.

In a way, Josh had been my best girlfriend even more than Rogers. He made much better suggestions for outfits, he knew what to wear, what to order at restaurants, the books to read before they became popular, what music to listen to before everyone else was talking about it. Now he had moved on.

This was something I had never tested out emotionally. I knew he'd go away to college. We were all going our separate ways in another year but I didn't know how it would feel. This was how it felt.

Changing my mind about returning to The Briar School was possible but I had made the right decision. Staying home was what I needed to do. I wanted to stay at the farm.

There was just this bump to get over.

After getting dressed for dinner, I went downstairs and found Lockie sitting at the kitchen table with Jules. He looked wonderful in a polo shirt, cotton sweater and navy trousers.

"You should come with us," I said, realizing she would be left alone.

"Thank you, that's very sweet but your father will be home in a couple hours so I'm on the job."

Whatever she had in the large pot was scenting the entire room with a delicious aroma.

"What are we missing," I asked pointing to the stove.

"Braised beef," she replied.

That was a family favorite we all loved and it made me want to call Josh and beg off, but he was expecting us.

"And?" I asked.

"Popovers."

"This is so unfair," I replied going to the door.

Lockie followed me to my truck and we began the drive to the restaurant two towns away. I didn't say anything because I wasn't sure if I started I would be able to stop.

"I got the horse sold, she'll be leaving tomorrow," Lockie finally said into the silence.

Good. I wanted a topic with no emotional component.

"That was fast. No trial period?"

"She's a horse with a lot of promise and they know what they want. They'll have their vet check her over, but she's fine and won't be coming home again. She'll get the job done for them."

"Everyone's happy then."

"Yes," Lockie replied. "Except for you."

"I'm happy," I insisted.

"That's news to me."

"I'm fine."

"Great. Why are we going to the Garnet Inn when there are so many restaurants closer?"

"There's a television show on the Gourmet channel and the host visits quaint inns around the country and he went wild about this one. He couldn't get over the artisanal goats milk soap in the rooms upstairs."

"I hope Jules saves some dinner for us," Lockie replied as I pulled the truck into a parking space and shut off the engine.

"The food is supposed to be excellent."

"Does everything have goat cheese in it?" He asked as we went to the front door.

"Yes, it sounded like it."

"Have you ever smelled a goat?"

"Order something else then," I replied as he opened the door for me and we entered the inn.

The maitre d' looked up.

"Joshua Standish's table," I said.

"Yes, his party is seated. Come with me."

The room was intentionally quaint with either real or fake antiques, old cracked oil paintings, and a florist shop's worth of late summer flowers. Josh and Paxton were at a table by the window and the last of the summer sun was visible through the trees.

Josh stood and gave me a kiss on the cheek as he always did. "Hi. I'm glad you made it. Hi, Lockie. How are you?"

"Fine, thank you."

"Talia, this is Paxton Teer. Paxton, this is the girl who got me through high school. Or most of the way," Josh added.

Paxton was exactly the type of guy Josh had been dreaming of for the last three years. With the body of an athlete, he was well-built with high cheekbones, a fine, aquiline nose and golden blond hair. Once discovered, Paxton was going to make his mark in show business, I had no doubt about that.

Josh finished making the introductions as we sat and had menus placed in front of us.

"At least goat's not on the menu," Lockie said after a quick perusal.

"No," I replied but noticed almost everything had goat cheese in it.

"Oh look, Talia," Lockie said. "Beet, arugula and pantysgawn cheese salad. I think I'll start with that."

He has just become a loose cannon. If he had wanted to

come to dinner, I felt Lockie had changed his mind and would have preferred to stay at the farm.

"Why don't you have the black cheese?" Lockie suggested. "It says here it's buried in soot to age."

"It says ash," I replied.

"I stand corrected. Either way you get a mouthful of burned wood."

Paxton closed his menu. "The black cheese has received rave reviews."

"Was it featured on the television show?" Lockie asked genially.

"Yes, it was," Paxton replied deep into being overly impressed with the status of the inn.

Josh and I looked across the table to each other. Lockie noticed.

"Paxton," I began. "Josh tells me you're an actor. Did you study or did it come naturally to you?"

"An actor must always study but I've been a performer since I was able to stand," Paxton replied and spent the next two hours recounting in minute detail every time he had gotten up in front of a crowd. We were an audience who couldn't escape.

All the courses were plated which meant artfully presented as if miniature still lifes. The squab was topped with micro greens and stuffed with chèvre, a French goat cheese. The dessert choices were between, unbelievably, goats milk ice cream, goat cheese cheesecake and a summer trifle made with goat mascarpone.

"Hmmm," Lockie said picking up his fork and digging into the three-bite size piece of cheesecake. "I don't know if I have room for this after that huge meal, but it looks so good, I'm going to try."

"As actors, we're always watching our weight. You two burn it off at the barn, I'm sure," Paxton replied giving Josh a smile.

I hoped it was genuine and not acting. There was a lot to like about Josh as a person but the family resources couldn't be missed by someone who didn't grow up with the same benefits. The Standishes were old money. They were society.

My great-grandfather Swope had come to America in steerage, with no money and had done well. We were well-off, there was no doubt, but the Standishes were on a different level entirely.

We finished our coffee and tea, and I looked around for the waiter. The sooner I got Lockie out of there, the better.

"I've got it," Josh said, standing and coming over to me. "It was really good to see you both tonight. We'll do it again."

"How about pizza next time?" I replied quickly before Lockie had a chance to say anything.

"Pizza sounds great." Josh kissed me on the cheek then looked at Lockie. "Is it okay if I still kiss her?"

"You didn't really ever start, did you?"

"Okay," I said. "Goodnight. It was nice to meet you, Paxton. You be sure to let us know if you're going to be on television."

"No, we wouldn't want to miss that," Lockie added as we all proceeded to the front door.

It was still raining.

"We'll have to make a dash for it," Paxton said.

"We wouldn't want to get wet," Lockie replied.

Paxton hurried down the steps and across the parking lot.

"I'll call," Josh said as he followed.

Lockie held out his hand to me. "Come on, Silly, let's go home."

I put my hand in his.

7

I PULLED THE TRUCK into the farm driveway. "Where do you want to go? Your place or mine?"

"I'm serious about dinner."

"I'm sorry. It was a meal fit for a Barbie doll."

We ran from the truck into the house where the lights were off in the kitchen but for one over the table. I heard the television on in the den and headed in that direction.

Jules turned away from the television. "Hi. How was dinner?"

"What dinner," Lockie replied.

"You ate, didn't you?"

"It was the Master Chef Grudge Match. They weren't normal size portions," I explained.

"Was it a tasting menu?" Jules was baffled.

"No, I think that's how much they thought we should eat."

"Everything was three bites."

"You can't be serious."

"It's true."

"There's plenty of food left over," Jules said standing. "I'll heat it right up." She touched Lockie's arm. "I'm so sorry."

"Where's Dad?" I asked as we followed her into the kitchen.

"He's upstairs. He was so tired after all that traveling, he decided to . . ."

"Work in bed for a couple more hours," I finished the sentence.

"No, I think he's tired." Jules began taking bowls and containers out of the refrigerator. "Tell me all about the boyfriend."

I didn't say anything.

Jules turned to us in confusion.

"Calling him a horse's ass would be an insult to horses," Lockie replied.

"I definitely need all the details," Jules said as she began heating dinner.

By the time we had reached dessert, we had finished the story as well.

"Is there any possibility you could be wrong? Some people are nervous in social situations and try too hard.

Maybe Paxton was so talkative because he wanted to make a good impression on Josh's friends."

"Yeah, no," Lockie replied.

Jules shrugged. There's a Maxene DeWinter marathon on the Classics Channel. Let's watch it and forget about Josh's love life."

"I wanted him to be happy," I replied putting my dishes in the sink.

"He has to make his own choices," Lockie said.

"We . . . we didn't make decisions without consulting each other."

"Were you married to him?"

"In a way."

"Well, you're divorced now. He's found a new main squeeze."

"I don't have anyone to talk to," I said without thinking.

"Talia," Lockie said sharply. "You're doing it again."

I stopped and turned to him. "What am I doing?"

"I'm here. Talk to me."

"Oh my God, I'm so sorry. I didn't mean it like that."

"Yes, you did."

I went into the den and sat on the sofa while Lockie stood to the side practically glaring at me. I patted the cushion next to me. "Sit."

Lockie didn't move.

"Please."

Lockie sat, but not close.

"I came here six years ago. In that time period I lost everyone I had a history with."

Jules entered with a tray holding a large bowl and assorted fruit juices on the table. "Excuse me?"

"Keep going, Tal, insult all of us," Lockie said.

"If you would like me to say I'm sorry your feelings are hurt, fine, I'm sorry, but that doesn't change the facts. I lost my mother. I never knew my father. Greer loathes me. Rogers has not been my best girlfriend, Josh was and now he's gone. I had experiences with him that neither of you shared with us."

"It's called moving on, Talia," Jules said.

"You had experiences with Butch that will never been repeated with CB," Lockie replied sensibly. "You create new experiences."

"You said you'd get me a new best friend."

"And you called me an idiot but I did."

He was right, of course. In the same way I took CB out on the trails and spent time building our relationship, I had to be willing to do that with Lockie. My reluctance came from fear of being hurt again, of losing someone close to me. I had tried to take care of Lockie, but still hadn't let him be my confidant.

"Will you pick out the dresses I should wear?" I asked him.

From the wing chair, Jules nudged me with her foot. "I'll do that."

Lockie smiled. "You know I'll just tell you they should be shorter and tighter."

"You're bad."

"You noticed."

"Is this over because the movie is starting and I want to see this one," Jules said.

"Why?" I settled back on the sofa.

"Maxene deWinter!"

"Who's that?"

"She was one of the most gorgeous film stars ever."

"If she's so gorgeous, why haven't I heard of her?" Lockie asked.

"Do you know who Anne Hathaway is?"

"No," Lockie replied.

I patted his leg. "Let's just watch the movie and we can see for ourselves if Maxene's any good."

The Clarion Pictures logo came on the screen, a trumpet against a stylized sunrise and the movie began. The story opened in a nameless large city and showed a tall office building. There was a dissolve to the inside, and it revealed a stenographic pool where secretaries were busily typing. There was a close-up of one secretary and Jules was correct, Maxene was a beautiful woman with delicate features and soft, wavy blonde hair framing her face.

It seemed that secretary was synonymous with escort as far as the boss was concerned and he either bribed or threatened his staff into going out on dates with his business customers.

"How is this movie a comedy," I asked.

"Seems okay to me," Lockie replied picking up a glass of juice.

"It is a little dated," Jules admitted. "But it's a pre-code movie."

"What's that?"

"In the early 1930's Hollywood told adult stories. Then the government cracked down with guidelines, a code, of what was appropriate. After that, there was a lot of fluff, separate beds, no sex, no innuendoes. Maxene made many movies in these early years that couldn't be made later."

"Now they make anything," Lockie replied.

"They seem to," Jules replied.

"Jules' father is in the film business," I told him before he got himself into trouble.

"Did I offend you?" Lockie asked.

"No. I'm in the food business. Besides, it's mostly the foreign rights end of things for my father. Sshh. Let's just watch."

Maxene was brought to a swanky dinner club by a handsome client with slicked back hair. There was a band playing and they danced to the music instead of eating dinner. He smiled almost all the time and she was uncomfortable. He tried to ply her with champagne, and she tried to beg off but her glass kept being refilled anyway.

"Stop making those tsk sounds," Lockie said to me.

"What is with her? Doesn't she get how he wants the night to end?"

"Yes," Jules replied.

"Don't get yourself into these situations," I said.

Jules pointed the remote at the television and increased the volume. "I can't hear the dialogue."

"Tsk. Well, finally," I said as Maxene pulled herself out of his grasp, rushed to the coat room, got her wrap and hurried out into the street. She stopped on the sidewalk and turned around.

"Talia, look at what's going to happen," Lockie said.

"Don't go back in the club!" I waved my arms at the screen.

Jules started to laugh.

"Hail a taxi! Leave! Go home."

Maxene stood there, the city zooming around her, wracked with indecision.

"Animal magnetism is impossible to overcome and she's in Epic Fail mode," Lockie said.

"No! No! She can do it!"

"Unh unh. She's giving in."

"You want her to go back inside."

"Sure I do, maybe he'll get lucky."

"Ugh!"

"Maybe she'll get lucky," Jules said.

"Not if it's with him!"

Maxene began to walk back to the club and the uniformed doorman opened the door for her.

"Dumb!" I shouted. "He's bad for her."

"Why? Because he wants to go out for dinner, and a twirl around the dance floor?"

"Yes."

Lockie looked at me in surprise.

"It's not that he wants to eat dinner, it's that he's using her for his own pleasure."

"Maybe this is fun for her too," Jules countered.

"For Bessie, it's a lark, for Maxene it's not. Some people you just can't keep from making mistakes. She'll be the one paying for dinner and I don't mean the check."

My father entered the den. "What's all the shouting?"

"I'm sorry, did we wake you?"

"No, I was working."

I looked over at Jules in my small triumph. "We're watching a movie about a stupid girl."

"She's not stupid. She's a little too trusting, perhaps," Jules replied. "You're welcome to join us."

"Since it is your house," Lockie added.

"Have some popcorn."

My father looked at the bowl. "It's blue."

"We don't eat enough blue food," Lockie said.

"It's naturally sweeter, only the hulls are blue. The kernels are white just like regular popcorn," Jules explained as she pointed out the colors.

My father sat in a chair and the three of us explained what the movie was about. Unfortunately, we each had our own version of the story and I was certain he was left knowing less than when he came in.

By the end of the movie, Maxene had been betrayed by this smooth-talker not once but twice and was still prepared to believe him when he said "I will never be completely happy again unless you marry me."

"Of course I'll marry you, darling," Maxene said.

And I threw popcorn at the television as the screen faded to black.

"That gives a new definition to the phrase 'dumb bunny'," I said standing up.

"Tali, she loves him," Lockie said.

"He's not worthy of her."

There was silence in the room.

I turned to my father. "I'm sorry. I didn't mean you."

He stood. "You're right about the movie and you're right about me but people can change. Even you can change, my adorable daughter." He kissed my forehead. "Goodnight, everyone."

I remained motionless for a moment unable to remember ever being kissed by my father before.

Greer walked in. "What's going on?"

"We just watched a movie," Jules replied.

"Why am I never included in these family gatherings?"

"Maybe if you acted like you were part of the family, you would be," I pointed out.

"Bitch."

I stared at her. "If you say that to me again, next time I'm going to haul back and hit you as hard as I can. Trust me, you'll be on the floor and it's not a threat, it's a guarantee."

Greer regarded me with her elitist arrogance. "Common."

I slapped her as hard as I would a horse fly sitting on CB's leg.

Coming from behind, Lockie put his arms around me, pinning my arms down. Jules jumped up and inserted herself between us.

"That's enough!"

"She hit me!" Greer shouted as she struggled to retaliate.

"And I'll do it again, gladly," I shouted back, trying to wrench myself from Lockie's grip.

He took my arm and dragged me out of the den, pushed me into the kitchen and blocked the way of returning.

"What is wrong with you?"

"She had it coming!"

"Never in my life have I hit anyone."

I shrugged.

"Would you hit a horse to train it?"

"No."

"You don't hit Greer to train her either." Lockie grabbed my hand, opened the kitchen door and pulled me outside.

"Where are we going?"

"I'm not leaving you in there with her. You think she's not going to be looking for you all night to finish what you started?"

"I started it? She called me a bitch."

"So what? You're not a bitch, and everyone knows that." He opened the passenger door of my truck. "Get in."

I stood there without moving.

"Get. In."

8

THAT'S WHY BIG HORSES PAID ATTENTION to what Lockie told them to do. He sounded like he meant it. I got in and he drove the short distance to the barn, then we went upstairs to his apartment.

"There's been something going on with you for a couple days now but you didn't want to confide in me. Tonight you will or we won't go to sleep."

"I don't really appreciate being told what to do."

"And why is that?" He sat on his couch.

"I've been on my own for quite a while now."

"Yeah, you're really on your own here at the estate."

"Do not start with the money."

"How do you define being on your own when everything you need, the best of it, is provided for you?"

"My father hasn't been around."

"And your mother is dead."

I glared at him.

"Say it. Your mother is dead."

I didn't say anything.

"So you're like an orphan?"

"I made my own decisions."

"With the help of the ex-husband."

"Lockie!" I couldn't believe he was speaking to me like this. "I'm out of here."

"You leave and tomorrow at first light I put Wing in the trailer and we leave."

"Why are you acting like this?"

"Why are you acting the way you are?"

"I didn't do anything to you!"

Lockie paused for a long moment. "You're not figuring this out."

"What?"

"You're not living your life."

"Of course I am."

"As someone who came very close to dying, I know you're not. You're on a hot walker going in circles. There's forward motion, but you're not going anywhere."

"I don't want to argue with you," I said and meant it.

"Argue with me. Fight me."

"I don't want to!"

My life seemed like one long fracas and I needed it to

stop. The only time I experienced peace was when I was out hacking a horse or laying down next to Lockie.

"That's the problem. That would require you experiencing some emotion."

"You don't know what you're talking about. I feel more than I can handle most of the time." I walked over to the large window that overlooked the pastures. It was too dark to see anything this late at night.

"And you don't do anything with it. You hold it inside like a personal treasure."

"That's not true."

"It is, Tal. You're practically submerged in the loss of your mother, the abandonment of your father, of being alone here with no one but Butch, a gay guy and a girlfriend who is preoccupied with her own feelings of inadequacy."

"You got it entirely wrong. I'm happy."

He didn't reply.

"I am happy," I insisted.

"You can't sleep at night. You can't concentrate on your riding. CB has done everything he can to woo you but you still can't connect with him. And you can't or won't connect with me. I don't see how that translates into happiness."

"You can't push me on this."

"Wrong. You must be pushed and since no one's done it before, I'm taking on the job."

"I'm doing this in my own time."

"You'll be doing it on my schedule now which means tonight," Lockie replied.

"No. I can't."

"You will."

"You don't do this with a horse. I've never seen you force one into doing anything."

"We never get to this point. They're trained to go along with me from the beginning."

"What about the lessons in small doses so they can be processed? You're demanding everything in one night."

Lockie shook his head. "That's because you are such a laggard. You have to play catch up."

"You wouldn't do this to Wing."

"Wing wouldn't force me."

"I'm not forcing you! This is all your idea."

"It really must be a big deal for you or you wouldn't be resisting me with such determination," Lockie said.

"I'm not!"

"Denying it doesn't make it so. I wish I knew what your mother would have said to you now because that's the only person you would listen to. I don't think she babied you. She didn't spoil you. Help me. Tell me what she would have said to you."

I walked back and forth in front of the window.

"I want to repaint this apartment and get you new furniture," I said.

"Thanks. Quit avoiding the issue. What would your mother have said?"

"She loved me, Lockie."

"Your father loves you."

"She made me feel loved."

"How?"

In danger of crying, I shrugged.

"Come here, Tali, sit by me."

I turned to him and Lockie nodded.

Walking over to him, I took his hand he held out to me and Lockie pulled me closer.

"What did she say to you?"

He put his arm around my shoulders and drew me to him, my head on his chest. At least I didn't have to look at him.

"She said 'I have been blessed to have you in my life.'"

"And then what else?"

"She would lie and say everything was going to be all right."

"Everything is."

"She never got better."

"I did."

"What does that have to do with it, Lockie?"

"That was the lifespan allotted to her. Death rushed up to me, so close its breath was my breath. For some reason I was given a reprieve."

"Are you saying that everything my mother had to do in this lifetime was completed?"

"I know she had enough time to raise a beautiful daughter who is enormously kind and compassionate."

"And? Aren't you going to list all my failings? How I've had a pretend boyfriend and slapped my sister and insult everyone?"

"No."

"I have disappointed everyone except my mother."

"I'm not disappointed."

"I don't believe you. We've been working for almost two months, I still ride dressage as if I'm riding hunter seat, I don't want to do the hunter pace, and I . . ."

"Came here when I needed you. That's what's important," Lockie said.

"No."

"You're going to tell me what's important to me?"

"If the fact that I showed up when you called me is so crucial, why are you so annoyed with me tonight?"

"I'm not. You're upset and you have been upset since the day I arrived and obviously long before that. You're so uncomfortable, Tal. I'm here to help you get through it."

"I don't think I can. This is what's normal."

"Then we'll retrain you."

"You said my mother didn't spoil me. She did. She thought I was perfect. There are times I think I will chase that the rest of my life, trying to duplicate that feeling of being so acceptable. But it's impossible. It was my mother and only she could see me as she saw me."

"I think you're perfect. I've never met a better you. Not anywhere."

I shook my head. "I'll disappoint you."

"We'll see who disappoints who first."

"How would you disappoint me?"

"I couldn't begin to imagine how and neither can you." He kissed my head. "Can we go to sleep now?"

"Yes."

We lay down on top of the quilt, he turned out the light and reached for my hand.

"Lockie, will CB forgive me?"

"He's crazy about you. He'd sit in your lap if he could. Go to sleep, Talia."

The next morning, the sun was trying to come out from behind gray clouds and my feet squished on the grass as I went to the house. When I opened the door, my father was at the kitchen table and Jules was making breakfast.

"I looked in your room, your bed wasn't slept in so I'm assuming Lockie's was."

I removed my boots. "On not in."

My father looked at me.

"We slept together but we didn't sleep together. Don't fire him."

"I can't very well tell you not to do what I've done. You're too old for that."

"You did with Greer."

"Rui was using her."

Greer entered the kitchen. "What makes you think Lockie isn't using the Virgin Vixen?"

The door opened and we all turned to see Lockie enter.

"Did I get here at a bad time?"

"No," my father replied.

"The crew just arrived to work on the outside course but they're bringing too much heavy equipment."

"It's not for the outside course, it's for the cottage."

"What cottage?" Greer asked.

"Lockie's. He should have a house. That apartment was never intended for long-term residency."

"Are you serious? He's staying? Staying permanently?"

No one said anything for a moment.

"Here's a suggestion, Greer. Eat, get dressed and go tack up your horse because you still have a lesson at nine," Lockie said.

"What would you like for breakfast?" Jules asked.

"I'll eat later," she snarled and left the room.

"What's this about a cottage?" Lockie asked as he sat at the foot of the table.

We each had our places by now. It made us seem like a family, and maybe we were becoming one.

"You need a house. I don't know why one wasn't built long ago. We had a caretaker here but he lived up the road and after my grandfather retired he lived here full-time."

"I didn't know that," I said spooning some raspberry and white peach preserves onto my plate.

"Your great-grandparents loved it here. My grandmother was a highly accomplished gardener. She could have been a landscape architect if she had been so inclined. The Howe Museum garden in town was designed by her."

"We'll have to go see that," Lockie said. "Jules, you'll come with us?"

I had a cup of tea lifted halfway to my lips and had to put it back down because I knew I wouldn't be able to swallow.

Jules sat next to me and pulled apart a morning bun. "Wouldn't you two rather be alone?"

Lockie had an expression of being completely surprised by the suggestion. "No, I don't think so. Do you, Tali?"

I shook my head. "No."

There was a knock on the door and Rogers came in. "Hi. It finally stopped raining so I wanted to get an early start."

"Would you like some breakfast?"

"No, I . . ." Rogers looked at my plate. "Maybe just a little."

"Sit down and help yourself," Jules said.

My father drained his cup of coffee then got up from the table. "Talia, you're starting with the tutor next week so create a schedule for your day before then. Lockie, if you're done, let's go talk to the contractors and make sure everything is the way you want it."

Lockie finished his tea and took his morning bun with him. "We'll have a group lesson at nine."

"I have to ride with Greer?" I asked.

"You always did before."

"I didn't," Rogers pointed out.

"It's a busy day," Lockie said as he followed my father outside.

"How am I going to have a lesson with Greer?" I asked putting my fork down.

"Try apologizing," Jules replied.

"What happened?" Rogers was spooning scrambled eggs and mushrooms onto her plate.

"I slapped her last night."

"No kidding? Wow. She'll never forgive you," Rogers said.

That was the truth. Greer was not big on the whole forgive and forget thing. In her life, she was stacking up real or imagined slights like cord wood. I shouldn't have slapped her and did feel remorse but also felt she been pushing me for years and had always gotten away with it.

This year could be different. We'd be going our separate ways, she was going to school and I was staying home. If I made a point of avoiding her, maybe she'd relax a bit. Without the stress of having to qualify for the National Horse Show or having to attract the attention of her riding coach,

Greer could focus on something that would make her happy.

I had no idea what that would be. What made me very happy was to know I'd be spending the next year at the farm instead of wasting time at The Briar School.

Lockie said I didn't have anything to make up to CB but that wasn't the truth. I had to do more with him, be a better friend. Let him sit on my lap.

We finished breakfast and Rogers drove us down to the barn, passing all the construction workers and the two bulldozers whose tracks were making a mess of the pastures.

"When is the outside course going to be completed?" Rogers asked.

"By the end of the week, I think. You're really looking forward to it?"

"I sure am."

"You hated riding."

"I love riding Karneval. Everything happens at the right speed with her. She doesn't get ahead of me. I don't feel like it's all spiraling out of control."

I nodded.

"I love Lockie," Rogers said. "I don't mean in that way," she added quickly. "Love him in a romantic sense. I mean he's such a good coach that I don't dread lessons anymore. He doesn't give me more than I can do."

Aren't you lucky? I thought as she stopped the truck by the barn and I got out.

We went into the barn and I continued down the aisle, avoiding the mucking in progress, and grabbed a couple carrots from the small refrigerator in the tack room. Butch was out in the pasture with the ponies with whom he seemed to have an affinity.

CB's nose was pushed as far as he could get it between the bars reminding me to speak to one of the workers and ask what it would take to get those removed. I opened the stall door and held out the carrot to him. "Bite," I said. He clamped his teeth down and I broke the carrot for him.

"I'm sorry. I'll do better." I put my arms around his neck.

Twenty minutes later Rogers and I were exhausted. Lockie had us ride without stirrups for the entire lesson and we weren't just doing a nice collected trot, he worked us until my legs were shaking. Greer was impervious to the session because she had to prove she was better than we were. That seemed to be true because when Lockie told us the lesson was over, I collapsed on CB's neck and Greer shrugged it all off.

"Don't leave the farm, Greer. You'll ride Spare after lunch," Lockie said as he went to the side door.

She glared at him.

"Do you think twenty minutes is enough?" Lockie asked.

"That's what you had them do."

"They're going to be working on a different program,"

he said. "You have a show in less than two weeks. Get serious about your riding."

"Do you think you can talk to me like that just because you're fooling around with Talia now?"

"No, I think I can talk to you like that because I'm your coach."

"You don't have to be."

"That's so true. Go find someone else," Lockie replied.

"Are you kicking me out of the program?"

"Yes."

"We'll see how long you last here after I talk to my father."

"Go. I think he's at the cottage site now," Lockie said as he left the arena.

9

GREER PRODDED COUNTERPOINT and they cantered out of the arena.

"Wow," Rogers said. "Is that what it's like here all the time?"

"No." I thought for a moment. "There's something going on with her."

"That's why you slapped her?"

"I did that because she called me a bitch one too many times."

We headed at a walk down the driveway to cool the horses off. At the open gateway, we turned into the field not only to avoid Greer on her way back, but to see what the progress was on the outside course.

The ruts from the bulldozer would have to be repaired

and the pasture reseeded before the end of October. That would give the new grass a good start for next year but it couldn't be done while it was still this warm out.

"Aren't you going to miss going to school?"

"No. How are you going to feel about galloping down this hill and having this banked jump in the middle?"

"I've seen worse on the hunt field," Rogers replied.

Going up the hill wouldn't be bad but leaping off the table Lockie had designed would be like becoming airborne. It was not something I wanted to do, even on CB who probably wouldn't notice it.

Rogers was holding her reins by the buckle in one hand. I had never seen her do that before.

"I feel like I found the magic stone and got a new life in a computer game," she said.

"Did you get special powers, too?"

"In a way, I did. Remember that game we used to play, *The Hidden Glen?*"

"Yes. How could I forget? We played it for hours in freshman year."

It was all about Ireland during the time of the Celts and the players had to make it through a dangerous forest before coming into the glen populated by dangerous beasts and spirits. There was a maze, too, if I recalled correctly. It was difficult and complicated to the degree that I finally gave up on it but Rogers didn't. Something about making it through the glen with two arms and two legs inspired

Rogers. It was devilishly hard to come out the other side without missing at least one body part.

It was possible to buy special powers but the cost was enormous, an eye or the player's sword hand. It was a game designed to be one skirmish after another. Not only were there the predictable adversaries, I had felt the game was fighting me, too. Once that occurred to me, it lost all its charm because it was too much like real life.

"What was the special power presented to you?" I asked as we went around the table jump.

"More bold than beautiful."

In the game, everything was a trade. No one was able to be both attractive and smart. The players were always left with one positive trait and one negative one.

"You may not be beautiful but you're cute."

"I look like Monsieur Bibendum."

"Who?"

"The Michelin tire logo. Round rolls, puffy. That's what I look like."

"Rogers, you do not."

"I've lost five pounds this summer."

"Good. Don't worry about what you look like, just concentrate on getting fit."

"Given the way Lockie works us, I don't think there's a choice. He wants me to jog in the evening."

"Seriously?"

"Yes."

"Are you going to?"

"I started. I can't run really. I walk fast and then slow down. It's pathetic."

"You need to build up your stamina."

"If Lockie can do it, I guess I can."

"What do you mean if Lockie can do it?"

"He runs in the evening after all the chores are done. He told me he runs on the trails, through the woods. Do you go with him?"

"No."

I didn't know he was running and my first instinct was to wonder if his doctor would approve. What if he fell in the woods? No one would know he was out there. What if he hit his head?

Then I realized I was just in nursemaid mode again. These were choices he had to make for himself. As much as I wanted him in bubble wrap, I had to accept that he wasn't going to live like that.

I just hoped he wasn't taking Wing out and trying the parts of the course that had been completed.

When we returned to the barn, Greer was just dismounting from Counterpoint.

"I hope you're happy."

"Thank you. I am," I replied truthfully, as I ran up my stirrup iron on the far side then throwing my leg over CB's neck and sliding to the ground. I ran up the stirrup on the near side. "What am I supposed to be so ecstatic about?"

106

"You're all against me."

"I'm not," Rogers said.

"What difference does that make?" Greer replied.

"You said everyone." Rogers lead Karneval into the barn.

I was shocked Rogers would talk back to Greer. It had never happened before.

"Lockie wants to help you. Pull on your big girl panties and do the work."

"He's getting paid to help me."

I wanted to say there wasn't enough money to make him stay here. "It's called a job." CB followed me into the barn.

"He doesn't help you because he's being paid," Greer shouted at me.

"He's the trainer at Bittersweet Farm. He's an extremely well paid babysitter."

Greer tossed Counterpoint's reins to Tracy and she strode down the aisle to where I had CB on the crossties.

"Lockie . . ."

"What?" I unbuckled the girth. Before I removed the saddle, I turned to Greer. "Rui didn't care about you. Lockie does. Why don't you try being just a little bit nicer to him?"

"So he's been complaining about me?"

I picked up the saddle. "No."

"I'll bet he has."

Lockie approached me. "What have I been doing?"

"Complaining about Greer," I replied.

"If I wanted to complain about you, I'd do it to your

face," Lockie said to her. "Why aren't you putting your horse away?"

"That's what Tracy is for."

"Tracy," Lockie called down the aisle. "From this point forward, you do not do Greer's work for her."

"Yes, boss," Tracy called back.

Greer flushed red, turned and hurried out of the barn.

"Your lesson this afternoon is going to be fun," I commented.

"I'm sure she's headed straight for your father's office to begin dictating terms. She's going to be so unhappy."

"I'll hose CB off and we'll go have lunch." I unclipped his halter from the crossties and began leading him to the wash stall.

"That's what I wanted to tell you. I'm going to town for lunch."

"Why?"

"The ex-husband called."

"Josh called you? Why?"

"He wants to have lunch and have a boy to boy talk."

"About me?"

Lockie kissed my cheek. "I will see you in about two hours." He began turning to leave.

"Wait."

He stopped and I stepped closer to him. I kissed his cheek.

"That is so much better," Lockie said with a smile.

Rogers watched him leave then looked at me. "Tal. You really like each other."

I shrugged.

"I don't think I've seen it before. My parents don't like each other."

"I like Josh."

"No, not in this way."

"Rogers, stop."

"Okay."

We started for the house.

"I'm happy for you."

* * *

When we entered the kitchen, I was introduced to my tutor, Amanda Hopkins. Over lunch, she explained the course work as listed on the pages she presented to me. It appeared to be roughly twice the amount of work in a semester at The Briar School. Rogers sat in stunned silence although she managed to eat the sandwich, fruit salad and delicate sable cookies Jules made for us.

"One other thing your father requested we begin this semester is to develop an organization or charity that benefits the community," Amanda added as she prepared to leave.

"What would that be?" I asked.

"Whatever you would like. It's an exercise in making an operation work, and learning how to manage funds. Start small. You don't have to build a hydroelectric facility."

"That's a relief," I replied being unable to imagine what kind of situation I was supposed to create.

"Think about it. We'll begin next week. It was very nice to meet you, Miss Kerr. I'm looking forward to working with you, Talia."

"Bye."

The thirty-something woman left by the front door and the three of us looked at each other.

"I'd bet my money that she's a Wharton Business School graduate," Jules said. "She probably has a couple degrees."

"Does she work for my father?"

Rogers took the course study out of my hand and began reading it.

"Yes. A house has been rented for her in Esophus. I saw a photo of it, it's really cute."

"Why wasn't a house rented for you?"

Jules was surprised. "How would I cook for you at two in the morning if I lived twenty miles away?"

"Right. Maybe you shouldn't be doing that, though. Your day doesn't have a beginning or end," I replied.

"This is exactly what I want to do."

"It's good to know."

"No wind is favorable if you don't know what port you're sailing to," Jules told me.

She was right and I was just beginning to know where I was going. Staying at the farm was a large part of it but with all the academic work expected and now this create an organization challenge, I would be lucky if I ever left the house.

My father hadn't stressed the importance of having a schedule for no reason. It wasn't likely I would be doing things by the hour but it would be crucial to block out portions of the time, otherwise I wouldn't know if I was coming or going.

Academic work would take up four hours of the day, which seemed like a cakewalk after being stuck in school for six, but I had twice as much to get done. Homework hadn't been a strain at The Briar School since I did just enough to get by, but that nonchalant approach wasn't going to work any longer.

Deciding what part of the day I most wanted to be at the barn was imperative. Summer was nearly over and the midday heat would be moderating soon. Riding early in the morning or in the evening wasn't as important as it had been. In another two months, we'd go off daylight savings, and it would be darker earlier. It didn't matter if I was going to ride in the arena but I didn't want to be out in the fields in low-light conditions.

"You know we have that hunter pace in a couple weeks," Rogers said. "Are you going to have time to train for it?"

"I don't know why we can't just go for a hack. Why do we need to train?"

"Because I would like to finish well. I don't want to come in with the rest of the hilltoppers."

Hilltoppers were riders with the hunt club who didn't jump, tended to take the easy trails and didn't go at a hunting speed.

The entire point of a hunter pace was to cover the course at the speed of a fox hunt, which meant quite fast and jumping whatever natural or semi-natural obstacles were in the way.

The last time I had been on a hunter pace was the first year I lived here and was teamed with Greer who had a horse name Carrena. For the whole two hours, we careena'ed around the countryside. Hating every minute of it, I swore never to subject myself to that kind of torture again.

Instead, Greer switched to equitation and I was dragged along for that. I wanted to ride, not compete. My entire life seemed like a test already and I didn't often feel as though I was passing. So, without much choice in the matter, I went along with Greer and my father. I had the lessons, went to the shows and made a small effort to do what was expected of me. I either rode Butch in the woods by myself or holed up in my room reading as much as possible. No one objected.

Until Lockie arrived. Then everything changed.

Except I still didn't want to compete. I wanted to accommodate Rogers since she was the only girlfriend I had, but galloping over trails through woods I had never seen before was hardly my idea of having fun.

"I didn't know we were supposed to win," I said as we walked back to the barn.

10

"I DON'T KNOW ABOUT WINNING but let's at least come close to the time," Rogers replied.

A team from the hunt club would ride the course days before the hunter pace. That time would be judged to be at the speed of a fox hunt. Teams would attempt to duplicate that pace and the one closest would win.

It wasn't a contest of skill and there was no way of knowing how fast or how slow the original team had gone. Those familiar with hunting, like Rogers, would have a better idea than someone like me who didn't attend hunts regularly. The whole event was more for fun than anything else, at least, that was how I saw it which was why I didn't see any point in rushing over hill and dale trying to match an unknowable time.

"What's the glory in coming close," I asked. "As long as you finish, isn't that good enough?"

"No."

"I thought you hated horse shows."

"I hate equitation. I'm never going to be a pretty rider like you."

"Excuse me? I'm not a pretty rider." It sounded like a doll with long nylon hair riding my sparkly plastic pony around the ring.

"You're very quiet and your position is perfect."

"Yes, exactly why I placed above Greer all the time. As if that ever happened."

"Greer performs. She's eye-catching. Do you remember that ice skater we used to watch who did that flip with her hand during her programs?"

Rogers and I loved ice skating. We sure weren't ever going to see equestrian events covered by television sports, so we had to watch something.

"I can't remember her name. Svetlana or something."

"Exactly. Greer is like the hand flip. She's showy. You're not and, no offense, but Butch wasn't helping you very much."

"Don't blame Butch for my shortcomings."

We stopped at the pasture and I could see Butch with his ponies. Somehow, I felt left out. We weren't best friends anymore. He was with his new buds. It was as it should be but I couldn't help missing what we had together.

"I'm not, but you're elegant and he's not. You're a different rider on CB. That's a match made in heaven."

That was a match made by Lockie.

Lockie, who always seemed to get it right.

"Thank you for the big vote of confidence and I appreciate the nice compliments even if I don't believe them. If I cross the finish line in one piece on this hunter pace, that's sufficient for me."

Rogers' look practically shot daggers at me. "Why can't you put a little effort into it?"

"I'm going, aren't I?"

"Why do you have to be dragged through everything?" She turned and continued to the barn.

"If you can explain that to me," I began.

"You're like a mule. You never do anything willingly. You take no pleasure in anything."

"That is so untrue."

"You loved being alone with Butch," Rogers replied. "What else?"

I thought for a moment.

"You can't come up with anything. Tali, my life's not perfect either. I've been bullied in school since kindergarten. I'm the fat girl in a universe of girls wearing size 1. At least when I was in the hunt field on Sarge, no one was judging me and I had fun. And, god knows, my parents were still asleep and my trainer wanted nothing to do with it because there are no prizes to be awarded."

"I didn't know."

"You didn't ask."

"Why did I have to ask, why didn't you just say something?"

"The same reason you never said anything. It doesn't get you anywhere. I'm so done with that."

I didn't know what to say. Good luck?

"Do you want to take CB out on the trails?"

"You're going out?"

"Karneval and I have to be fit and that applies to you, too. We're not going for a Sunday stroll. You canter most of the way on a hunter pace."

"Do you walk the rest of the way?"

"No, you're trotting or galloping to make up time."

"Swell."

"Okay, so you're not going?"

"No, I want to wait for Lockie."

"Fine. I'll see you later."

Someone else I just disappointed. I knew the expression.

The contractor who was building the outside course came out of the barn as Rogers was going in.

"Hi," I said to him. "I wonder if you could look at something I need done."

"I'm supposed to be up on the hill."

"This will be fast, I promise."

He followed me into the barn and I stopped at CB's stall

and pointed to the sliding door. "I want these bars to be removed."

"They're bolted in."

"Yes."

"You'll need a piece of angle iron to cover the bare surface."

"Okay. Can you do that?"

"When do you want it done?"

"Right now if possible."

"Which stall is the most important? I'll do that now and the rest later when I have the angle iron. Are you sure?"

"I'm sure."

"Let me get my power drill and it would be good to move the horse." He went down the aisle while I went into CB's stall.

"You're going to be so happy!"

* * *

About an hour later, Lockie entered the barn and saw CB hanging his head over the stall door. "What happened here?"

I stopped brushing Memento, a horse that Lockie had bought to sell about two weeks before. He was a cute round, brown gelding, barely larger than a pony and would be perfect for a young girl moving up from jodhpurs to breeches. The problem with this gelding was he had come from a stable where they weren't as concerned with technique as they should have been.

Lockie's had created a crash course to get him up to speed by instilling the basics with lots of flat work to start, as well as perfecting his transitions and balance. Someone was going to be a very lucky girl.

"CB said he wanted to look out."

"All right. How about we leave the bars on a couple stalls at the end of the aisle? It's not so much that they can reach the horse in the stall next to them but some may have bad habits about traffic in front of their stall."

"We had a horse like that, that's how we wound up with the bars. But it's too much like jail, Lockie."

"You don't have to convince me. Let's store the bars in the tractor barn, though, and not throw them away."

"In case."

"Yes."

"Fine. How is Josh?"

Lockie went into the tack room and I followed him.

"Lockie. How is Josh?"

"He's fine."

It didn't seem like that to me. "What did you talk about?"

"We had a man to man talk. Apparently he doesn't have any men in his life."

"What are you saying? He has a father, a brother and a boyfriend."

Lockie turned away from the bridle hung on the cleaning hook. "But they aren't unbiased."

"You're unbiased? Why does he need that?"

"Because he does and don't grill me because Josh asked me not to tell you what we talked about."

"It's a secret?"

Lockie removed the bridle from the hook. "Is saying something in confidence a secret?"

"Yes."

"Then it's a secret. Are you riding Memento this afternoon?"

"I wasn't going to."

"Then I will."

"Where's Tracy?"

"I think she's going to the dentist."

"What's up with Josh that it has to be a secret from me? I'm his best friend."

"I don't want to rub it in, Silly, but you were his best friend."

I stood there.

"What?" Lockie asked.

"Rogers is ticked off at me, Josh doesn't consider me his best friend anymore . . ." I turned away then turned back. "And you know what happened just after lunch?"

"What?"

I tried to say the words.

"Talia, what happened?"

"I stopped by the fence and Butch didn't acknowledge me. He was busy with the ponies. He's never ignored me before."

Lockie put his arm around my shoulders, pulled me near and pressed his lips to my cheek.

"He wasn't ignoring you. He probably didn't see you. Maybe he needs prescription eyeglasses."

Lockie stepped away but I grabbed his hand.

"Everyone's leaving me."

He smiled. "No. I'm not going anywhere and CB is still waiting to sit on your lap."

I turned and saw CB watching us while chewing a mouthful of hay, dropping half of it on the aisle.

"I don't like changes."

"Is that what your problem is? I'm glad we've defined it. Are you going to ride Memento for me or not?"

"Yes."

"Switch the egg-butt for a full cheek snaffle for today's ride."

"Why?"

"To change things up. Give him something to think about."

~ 11 ~

I SLAMMED THE LID DOWN on my laptop. Even with no photos, I knew what it look like.

"This freaking day . . ." I started.

Jules looked up from finishing a dessert she was creating. "What's wrong with today?"

I shook my head.

The door opened and Lockie entered. "I have to go look at a horse, do you want to go with me?"

"No, thank you."

I didn't want to look at another horse with an unpredictable future.

Jules put down the knife she was holding. "I think I have to go count the angels on the head of a pin."

"How long will that take?" I asked.

"Until you two sort out whatever is going on." Jules left the kitchen.

"What happened? You had a good ride on Memento. Rogers didn't try to run you over with her car when she left. You came up to the house and now this mood."

"I don't want to go look at the horse with you."

"Okay. I'll ride him."

"Where's Tracy?" I asked.

"Doing chores."

"I'll do her chores and she can go with you."

"No one is going anywhere until you tell me what this is about."

I didn't look at him.

"I can wait you out." Lockie sat down.

I started to get up and he put his hand on my arm.

"Are you angry with me? Because I don't know what I did."

"Let it be. Don't you have an appointment you have to get to?"

"I'm a highly paid babysitter. Isn't that what you told Greer today? If you two would stop screaming at each other maybe the entire town wouldn't know your business."

Lockie was relentless, goal-oriented and focused in a way I would never be. It was like being caught in a tidal wave of his determination.

"If I am a babysitter, what do I have to do, take you to

the playground and push you on a swing until you're in a better mood?"

"Can't you leave me alone for the rest of the day?" I just wanted to mourn the death of this unknown horse by myself.

"I'll make a deal with you. Tell me what's going on and I'll leave you alone for as long as you want."

Hope for a couple hours to myself.

I opened the laptop and turned the screen to face him.

He read for a moment, pressed the off button and the screen went dark.

"Accidents happen."

"This was an unnecessary accident."

I had been reading the news in the Equine Gazette online. A young woman, my age, was riding her horse over an oxer. The horse's front legs caught the rails. He flipped over the fence, landed badly and died from the injuries. The rider walked away.

I hated these stories. "It's unfair," I said.

"You wanted her to get hurt, too?"

"Of course not. He didn't ask to jump the fence. We should leave to them to their own lives. That's a pretty high price to pay for her to have some fun or glory or whatever she gets out of it."

Lockie stood. "No one's making you ride. If you don't want to, don't."

That wouldn't solve anything.

"Explain it to me. Why do you have to take such chances?"

"I don't know, Tali. Why do people do anything? Because it's enjoyable, it satisfies something in their lives."

"But not the horses."

"We've covered this before and we disagree. I couldn't force Wing to do anything."

I stood up so fast I knocked the chair over. "You're deluding yourself. In a very methodical way, over years, a horse is trained to perform whatever tasks are required. They're being taken advantage of."

"That's why they quit in front of fences every damn day, because they're automatons. You will not be able to train the swish out of CB no matter how hard we work at it. Have you ever watched the dressage tests at the Olympics? These are some of the most highly trained horses on the planet. Isn't that right?"

"Yes."

"In the last Games, I watched Calise intentionally miss a flying change, then he bucked, invented a gait I'd never seen before and headed for the exit. It's up to you to explain that."

"Simple. He was unhappy."

"I thought you said they are forced into doing exactly what we demand of them. It can't be both ways. They can't have free will and be submissive, too."

"You can't control anything a hundred percent of the time," I replied.

"Yeah, that's why someone came up with the word accident."

"If a skydiver jumps out of a plane and his parachute doesn't open, it was his choice to take the risk."

"And it was my fault I got thrown into the berm."

I reached for his hand. "I didn't mean that."

"You did and it was my choice. I knew the risks then and I know them now."

"Horses don't, Lockie. That's what I'm saying."

"And I'm saying this is a choice for them. I once had a horse who would pretend to be lame. They don't have to cooperate. I know you don't want to believe it but they want to be in a partnership with us. You should see the look on CB's face when you come down the aisle. He doesn't look like that for me."

"If that's true . . ." I started.

"It is," Lockie said over me.

"Then I owe him. He should be treated with dignity."

"He is. You had the bars removed from his stall. He poops and you run in there with a manure fork. The racetrack hay is imported from Canada. He's got a great life."

"Others are not that lucky."

"No, they're not but you can only take care of whoever is put in your path. You learned the wrong lesson from your mother's death."

"Don't go there."

"Watch me. You learned to fear loss when she was trying to help you become a warrior."

"You know this without knowing my mother, by only knowing me for a couple months?"

Lockie nodded and squeezed my hand.

"I don't believe you."

"What do you lose if I'm right?"

I shook my head. I didn't know if I wanted to scream or cry. Whatever it was, was right at the high watermark and in another minute the emotions would submerge me.

"You can only lose everything in your life that doesn't work anymore. Don't fight to keep it. Fight for something worthy of you."

I waved my hand and his through the air.

"Come here, Silly."

Lockie pulled me closer.

My face against his chest, I was enveloped by him. It was as though an eraser had been taken to the outlines of our selves.

* * *

We went to the farm in Killiam, bought the horse without either of us riding him, brought him home and turned him out in the pasture with the run-in shed.

There was a moment as Lockie turned from the gate, the sun was near the horizon but hadn't yet set, the light was

126

golden and he looked like all that was good. I was mesmerized.

"What, Silly?"

I put my arms around his neck and he put his arms around me.

"Are you really just a highly paid babysitter?" I asked.

He didn't reply.

"Don't answer. It doesn't matter."

Lockie laughed. "Of course it matters and I'm not. Are you capable of finding something wrong in everything?"

"No."

"I love it when you lie to yourself."

"Why?"

"You're such a bad liar."

I wanted to stay there forever but instead we went back to the house.

* * *

It was just as well Lockie hadn't bothered to enter Greer into the first jumper class of the day because she was out late, overslept and I was in charge of getting her in gear. She, of course, took a shower shouting at me the entire time.

"Tick tock, Greer. If you aren't ready by eight, we're staying here."

"Did he tell you to say that to me or are you making it up?"

She stepped out of the shower.

"Lockie said it. You have a class at ten and it will take an hour to get there."

"Where are we going?"

"Middlebury."

"Martie Wyrick's barn?"

"Yes. So?"

"I didn't know."

"How could you not know?"

Greer shrugged then pulled on her panties followed by tugging on her breeches.

We argued about nothing all the way downstairs where Jules handed me a large picnic basket that weighed a ton.

"You shouldn't eat the food on the show grounds," she said.

"So you're giving me enough to feed everyone?"

Jules kissed me. "I don't know how long this will take."

"We should be home in time for dinner," I replied going out the door.

Greer glared at Jules. "Yeah, I don't want to kiss you either."

Jules laughed.

This day was going to go on record for having the longest morning in history.

Counterpoint was standing on the aisle as we entered the barn.

"He's not groomed," Greer said as grabbed his tail dotted with pine shavings.

Lockie came out of the tack room. "I told you to take care of your horse. Did you think I was kidding?"

"Yes."

"I wasn't."

"You can groom him at the show," I said.

"He needs a bath."

"You should have done that yesterday and put a sheet on him overnight," Lockie replied as he went to the truck. "Are we going or not?"

"Tal, are you going to help me?" Greer asked.

"No," Lockie replied.

"Let her answer for herself!" Greer shouted.

"We have rules in this barn. I'm sorry if you don't like them but we all adhere to them."

"On whose say-so?"

"Your father gave me autonomy over the barn," Lockie said. "Smile or as close as you can get to it and we'll leave for your horse show. Otherwise, Talia and I have plenty to do here today. Your choice."

Greer unclipped Counterpoint, lead him out of the barn walked him up the ramp to our van secured him inside.

"You follow us in your car," Lockie told her.

"Why?"

"Because you might want to leave before we do and I

don't want to hear you whine for an hour." Lockie got in the truck's cab.

I got into the passenger side as fastened the seat belt as we drove up the driveway.

"This shouldn't be perceived as questioning you . . ." I started.

"But you're going to question me."

"Yes. Why are you treating her this way?"

"I would treat you the exact same way if you behaved like that. I used to run the barn for a man in Santa Barbara. What a great ranch that was. Right on the ocean. There's not much ocean property on that part of the coast, but he owned most of it. His daughters were a lot like Greer. Worse in some ways."

"How could you be worse?"

"Because all their friends were movie stars, or the children of celebrities. There's a private school but it's more of a holding pen. These kids are required to attend school so they go there. The facility is an old estate in Montecito and they learn everything they need to know to navigate the world in which they will live."

I thought about it for a moment. "You thought we were like that."

"I did."

I looked at him.

"Why wouldn't I? I thought it was the same situation

but on the East Coast. I was happy to get anything after the accident."

"We were your only job offer?"

"Pretty much. You know I came to Bittersweet with some medical issues. Your father was very generous and I continue to be very grateful."

"That's nice but I feel worse and worse about this."

Lockie smiled. "Why?"

"You thought you were going to be training two more brats."

"The last two brats, as you call them, both made it to the Nationals."

"So it was a disappointment coming here."

"Tali, you're doing it again."

"What?"

"Seeing the worst in everything."

"I wasn't even polite that first day."

"You were adorable and funny and I thought what a lucky guy I was to have found such a terrific place to live."

"Did you really?"

"Yes."

I didn't believe him because that's not how I would have felt.

"I'm sorry I was so rude that day."

"I think you apologized already."

"I'm still sorry."

"Why were you rude?"

"I had seen Greer with Rui the week before. All spring, it had been one upset after another. You walked up to the house so handsome and I could predict the future."

"You thought I was handsome?"

"Yes."

"Silly!" Lockie reached over with his hand and touched my arm.

"You know how good looking you are."

"Then I'm lucky I fell on my head and not my face!"

"Please. I hate thinking about that day." It made me queasy to imagine Lockie being thrown into that berm of earth and logs.

"You weren't there."

"You were barely there."

"After the fall, I sure wasn't."

"How were you the day you arrived at Bittersweet?"

"That was a long day of driving. I had a headache for the last six hours of the trip, and found the apartment, you said I would. I lay down and tried to sleep it off because I knew you two had lessons first thing in the morning."

"If you didn't feel well, no one would have held it against you."

"Tal. You would have."

Looking out the window for a long time, I decided maybe Greer was right about me. Maybe I did have the capacity to be a bitch. My mother would have been very displeased to see me act the way I had over the past year.

"You have an enormous capacity for patience," I said to him.

Lockie turned the van down a road and there were already trailers lining the road waiting to be directed into the field with parking.

"Everyone comes along at their own speed."

12

A STABLE HAND wearing an orange vest pointed down the field and we followed a four-horse trailer to the end of the rows. It was well into the morning and most of the competitors had arrived at dawn. Lockie parked and shut off the engine.

Greer pulled up alongside of the van and jumped out of her car. "We're hell and gone from the rings."

"What difference does it make to you? It's not like you'll have to walk over there like we do."

"Next time, assuming there will be a next time, wake up when you're supposed to," Lockie said. "We did the chores, took showers, had breakfast, and were still waiting for you to drag yourself out of bed. Now you're complaining that we're parked at the far end of the field?"

Greer paused. "No."

"Thank you. Get your horse out of the van, tack him up, get on and come over to the warm up area. Your first class was scheduled for ten and that's soon. I'll go get your number and have a look at the course."

Lockie began walking toward the barn and indoor arena.

Greer stood there for a moment.

"What's wrong?" I asked.

"I haven't been to an unrated show in years."

"You have to start your jumper career somewhere."

"I was supposed to be at the National."

"You're riding jumpers now and that's perfect for you."

Greer started up the ramp. "Will you help me clean Counterpoint up?"

Lockie didn't want her to get any help.

"I'll owe you."

"Not every interaction between people is quid pro quo. You don't have to buy me off. If I help you it's because you . . ."

"Is the word you're looking for incapable?"

"No, it's not."

I thought about what my mother would have said. People make mistakes. Even with the best intentions or efforts. That's the way life is.

"Let's just get it done so you can get to the ring before you miss the class."

"He'll know you helped."

I nodded. Yes, Lockie would know.

Fortunately, jumpers weren't braided for shows except at the upper levels, and Counterpoint's mane had been pulled recently. After Greer removed the shavings from his tail, and gave it a quick brush, he looked quite respectable even if a little rough around the edges.

We got him tacked and Greer into the saddle in under five minutes and I followed her toward the crowds. There was a bottleneck at a gateway and we had to pause for a moment.

"I know I'm the last person you want to take advice from but I'll give it a try anyway. Just do whatever Lockie tells you to do. I know you can."

The way cleared in front of us and Greer trotted off without saying anything.

I found Lockie, predictably, by the bulletin board where the diagrams for all the courses were posted and slipped my hand into his.

"They don't have the course up yet so we can't walk it," he said squeezing my hand.

"I helped Greer."

He leaned over and kissed my cheek. "Of course you did. I expected that."

"You said she had to do it by herself."

"That would have been better. She'll learn." He pointed to the sheet to our left. "Look at this line, Tali. Greer will actually need to be awake to make this turn."

"I thought this was supposed to be easy."

"You can't have a baby jumper class that goes twice around the outside. The fences aren't that big."

I studied the diagram more closely. "Is that a bounce combination?"

"Yes."

"What's that doing in a small show?"

"It's there as a learning experience."

A bounce was a no-stride combination. The competitors would jump the first fence and immediately be confronted by the second without a stride between the two.

In this case, the first fence was a plain vertical and the second was an oxer, two sets of jump standards placed close together with rails at the same height creating a spread fence. That was going to require the right speed and enough impulsion to be able to power over the oxer.

"When are they going to set up these fences?"

"As soon as the equitation over fences class is done."

"Are they going to give everyone a chance to walk the course?"

"There will be ten minutes. Let's go find her in the warm-up area."

"I told Greer to do everything you asked her to do."

He squeezed my hand. "Was that for me or for her?"

"For me!"

Greer was cantering in a large circle at the edge of the field because there were about a dozen kids on horses under varying degrees of control jumping the practice fence. She saw us, slowed to a trot and came toward us.

"This is a madhouse out here," Greer said.

"Is he warmed up?"

"I haven't jumped him."

Lockie glanced over to the swelling crowd of ponies and horses racing around in the warm-up area. "That's fine, don't worry about it. The fences aren't that big."

Greer was about to protest, glanced toward me then shook her head slightly.

"We need to get to the in-gate," he said and we began walking in that direction.

Mothers were hurrying after children, trainers were looking for riders, and two young girls were chasing a loose pony still wearing its stable sheet and leg wraps. I felt like a time traveler in my own life. Any one of these young riders could have been me.

I watched as a pony hunter over fences class was pinned and the winners exited.

Lockie pushed Counterpoint's head in the direction of the other ring. "Go into the hunter ring and pop over the first two fences," he told Greer.

"What?"

"Quick."

"They'll be angry," Greer said as she snaked her way through the waiting jumpers.

"So what?"

I followed them and Greer trotted through the open gate.

"Miss!" The ring steward noticed someone had entered and was heading toward the fences. "You can't do that! You must leave!"

Lockie walked up to the man who shook his head vigorously. Lockie kept talking as Greer jumped all the fences around the outside of the ring then trotted out the exit.

Lockie smiled and left the ring. "Go to the in-gate!" He called to Greer and she made her way through the crowd.

"I thought you were trying to be a good influence on her."

"It's easier to apologize than to ask for permission," Lockie replied. "We're here to win, aren't we?"

"No, we're here to school."

Lockie kissed my cheek, took hold of my arm and propelled me to the jumper ring. "You're so cute."

Reaching the gate, the crew was moving standards around and a tractor was leaving by the out-gate having deposited a roll-top jump at the far end of the ring.

Greer slid off Counterpoint and handed me the reins. Lockie looked at her.

"Would you please hold him for me?"

"Yes, I will."

Lockie and Greer as well as many other trainers and riders teams entered the ring to walk the course. The purpose was to discuss how each jump should be taken, from what angle, and how many strides the horses would have between the fences.

This was far more preparation than I had ever done with Butch, who I depended on to figure it out for himself.

Along with his sunglasses, Lockie was wearing dark jeans, our stable colors polo shirt and mahogany paddock boots. He rarely wore a baseball cap because he said he was neither a baseball player nor a kid. Always neat, always clean, always the consummate professional, Lockie had transformed our backyard barn into a show stable in a way that no one else had.

Rui had treated the farm as if it was a vacation spot. He showed up late for lessons, slept in, didn't come home and left Pavel and Tracy to take up the slack. His music was loud and so was he. He was a good rider, a good trainer and a lousy coach, but we had a reputation and not very many people wanted to deal with Greer.

Mellissa from Canada made sure the word was spread throughout the show circuit that Greer was vile and I was uncooperative. Anything said will always come back to you, sooner or later, and I had heard her litany of complaints. It was not as though Mellissa wasn't paid extremely well for the ten days she managed to hang on.

In a way, it was understandable why Greer chased her off. Mellissa hadn't possessed the most sunny of personalities even before she knew us.

I was glad she was gone. I was glad they were all gone.

Pulling a piece of carrot out of my pocket, I held it out for Counterpoint and he crunched it into small pieces that dotted his lips orange. I wiped his mouth with the bottom of my shirt.

The riders and trainers left the ring and the ringmaster called for the first entrant as Lockie gave Greer a leg up.

"Check your girth," he told her.

"I checked it earlier."

"Check it again."

She was able to tighten it one hole.

"Have you memorized the course?" Lockie asked.

"Yes."

"Repeat it to me."

"Plain rails to the brush, tight corner to the oxer, straight to the wall, right turn down the line to the cross rails, the in and out, turn, take the wall from the opposite direction, over the roll-top, the hanging panel, and finish with the plain rails."

"Good girl."

The steward called her number and she entered the ring.

"If she can just hold on and steer, she'll be fine," Lockie said.

The fences were lower than anything she schooled over at home. These were in the three-foot range. Obviously, Greer could not take a jumper to a show and pop over novice fences, as it wouldn't be fair to the other horses and riders. She might have been there for practice but it had to be at her level and by the look of the horses around me, there was serious competition.

This wasn't going to be a cakewalk for her. The oxer had quite a spread, the roll-top was formidable and the wall looked to be three feet but had a rail on top of it. There was nothing she hadn't jumped before, but riding at a show with another ring nearby and the loudspeakers, kids screaming, horses, trucks, fabric flapping in the wind and drinks cups skittering across the ground made it difficult for horses to concentrate. This was the first time Greer had shown Counterpoint and she really didn't know what to expect.

I found myself holding my breath as she headed for the first fence.

"It's okay, Tal," Lockie said as he glanced over at me.

He didn't know what kind of mood Greer could be in if she had a bad ride.

"She didn't practice enough."

"She did or I wouldn't have brought her."

Counterpoint cleared the first fence easily and they galloped to the brush. There was plenty of air under them. They landed, she looked for the next fence and made the turn.

A minute later Greer had completed a clean round and was walking through the out-gate as we went up to her.

"Good job, Greer. How did he feel?"

"He got a little forward coming down the center line."

"I saw you sit back," Lockie replied.

"He's strong."

"We'll work on it. Take him to the other side of the hunter ring and walk him around until the class is pinned."

Greer nodded and left while we stood by the rail and watched the rest of the entrants go. There were many competent riders and talented horses but it was a challenging course and no one else had a clean round.

I had to admit Greer knew how to ride. She wasn't just sitting there like some of the equitation riders we knew. She was making the transition from hunters into jumpers within weeks instead of months. In large part that was due to Lockie's training and finding her the perfect horse.

The horses who placed were called back into the ring and a blue ribbon was attached to Counterpoint's browband. Greer cantered halfway around the ring and left. We saw her head toward the van to take care of Counterpoint.

"Are you hungry? Do you want lunch?" I asked Lockie.

"Yes and yes but I need to talk to Hank Faustino about Memento so I'll meet you at the van."

I nodded and made my way through the crowd.

Counterpoint was untacked and in the van when I arrived. Greer was sitting on the ramp shredding the ribbon.

She looked up at me. "I know what you're doing."

"What am I doing?" I had no clue what she was talking about.

"The two of you."

"Yes?"

"You're trying to make me feel good about myself."

"Why do we need to do that? You just won the class."

She pulled the rosette apart. "He keeps saying stuff like 'good girl'."

"You did a good job. What would you have him say?"

"Counterpoint was just better than the other nags."

"No. You had some real competition out there and you followed Lockie's instructions to a tee. Counterpoint couldn't have done it without you."

She didn't look at me. "Derry's going back to Ireland. He's going to try out for the team."

"I didn't know."

"How could you not know?" Greer dropped what was left of the ribbon on the ramp.

"Derry didn't tell me."

"He told Lockie."

"Lockie didn't tell me."

"Derry was like 'See ya, Fluff.'"

"Excuse me?"

Shrugging, Greer didn't look at me. "Dollface."

That was rude in itself.

I didn't know what I was supposed to say since Derry wasn't in my Top Ten list of anything. Taking Greer into the hayloft and laying her out on a horse sheet was hardly my idea of a romantic interlude. Seeing an opportunity, he had taken it but Derry could have been a better man than that.

If I said she was well rid of him, that could be wrong and if I said Ireland wasn't that far away, that could be wrong, and the truth was, I didn't realize she cared about him so nothing said was giving me any hints. Maybe the rules were that Greer was always the dumpor and didn't know how to handle being the dumpee. That was believable. That Greer had been in some kind of love with Derry, was not believable.

"You could go to Ireland for Winter Break."

"He doesn't want to see me again. He says I'm too high-strung. He prefers Irish Thoroughbreds."

"He's got something against American Thoroughbreds?" I was really starting to dislike this guy.

"Narrow through the chest and scatty."

Narrow through the chest implied no room for a heart, no room for lungs to insure stamina. I couldn't imagine how Derry could have insulted her more than that, although I could think of a couple comments that might come close.

"Then we should be glad he's gone."

"Yeah. Men are like buses, right?" Greer stood.

That's what her mother, Victoria, said. If you miss one bus another comes along in fifteen minutes.

That's not what my mother said so I didn't think I should agree with Greer.

Considering the kind of woman Victoria was, it was no surprise Greer turned out the way she did.

"My mother married Dad for his money," Greer said brushing off her breeches. "He was the bus that came along at the right time."

If I said Victoria could often be found on the street so would have more than a passing familiarity with buses and anything else, that would hardly be a welcome comment so I decided to keep quiet.

"Why did your mother marry him?"

"So I would be taken care of," I replied. That was the standard answer.

"I think she loved him," Greer said.

So shocked, I was speechless for a moment.

"He loved her," Greer continued.

"I'm sure of that."

"Do you think he loved my mother?"

As I struggled to find the right thing to say, Greer stopped me. "Don't bother. Even I don't like her very much."

Lockie came around the end of the van and looked at us, then down at the destroyed blue ribbon. "What's going on?"

13

"WHY DIDN'T YOU TELL ME Derry's going back to Ireland?" Greer asked.

"When is this happening?"

"Soon."

"He didn't tell me," Lockie said. "We'll have to find someone else to ride Counterpoint. Are we having lunch?" He opened the driver's side door to the van and dug around in the side pocket until he found his pill bottle.

I went to the cooler, opened it and took out a bottle of water. "Greer, would you move the chairs into the shade?"

We had folding chairs in our stable colors and Greer began to move them so the van would offer some shade.

Jules packed everything we'd require for a gourmet picnic, from utensils to strong plates, sandwiches, a variety of salads and cookies for desserts. Underneath it all, I discovered a small stash of handmade caramel filled chocolates she knew I loved.

I handed Lockie his plate. "If you don't feel well, take Greer's car and go home."

"You don't feel well?" Greer asked him.

"He has a headache," I said.

"You didn't say anything about it," she said leaning over to him.

"Too much sun."

"Why aren't you wearing a hat? I have one in my bag," she said and left to get it.

"What happened to the ribbon?"

"It fell apart," I replied.

Greer came around the van and plopped the baseball cap on his head. "Didn't anyone ever tell you you're supposed to wear a hat in the sun?"

Lockie positioned it on his head. "Thank you, Greer." He took a pill and a drink of water, then a bite of sandwich.

"It's so bright today that when I made the turn up-sun, for a moment I couldn't see the fence," she said.

"You did a good job but the next class is going to be more challenging. It'll be timed, the fences are bigger and they're combining it with another jumping class."

"Can they do that," I asked.

"There were no complaints when they asked us."

"No one asked me," Greer pointed out.

"Do you object?" Lockie asked.

"Should I?"

"I think you're the best jumper team on the grounds so you won't have any trouble with it."

"You're just saying that," Greer snapped back.

"For what purpose?"

"So I'll be acquiescent," she replied.

"If that's how other people treat you, that's not how I treat you. I'm here as your coach, as your trainer, not your nanny. I don't have a pacifier in my pocket."

Greer gave him a look. "You didn't have a hat either."

"Correct. There's a show over into New York State in three weeks. Decide if you want to do that."

"Are we going to show a couple times a month?"

"Do you still want to go to Florida this winter? If so, yes."

Since nothing had been said about Florida for a while, I had felt as though the issue had been dropped. If Lockie left, then I'd have to oversee the barn. They'd be gone most of the winter.

"I'm not sure," Greer replied. "There will always be shows around here."

"That's true."

"It would be nice to spend the winter down south."

I nodded.

"We'll have to make the arrangements," Lockie pointed out.

"But I'd be there alone for three months," she said.

Lockie looked at me.

"Jules sent some cookies for us and lovely chocolates. Does anyone want either or both?" I said standing up.

"My class is right after the lunch break." Greer took her plate and went around to the other side of the van.

Putting my hand on his shoulder, I reached for his empty plate. "Do you feel any better?"

"My headache is almost gone but now I learn I'm invisible."

I tapped the bill of the cap. "Not to me."

* * *

When we reached the in-gate, the grounds crew had just finished setting up the course. The fences appeared to be about three-feet-six and the course was designed to be a challenge even more than the morning's class.

Greer came up behind us leading Counterpoint. "I've never ridden a timed course before."

"Don't worry about the speed. It's practice."

"Are you for real? Do you actually go into a class and think it doesn't matter if you don't win?"

"Yes, Greer, I actually do," Lockie replied.

She shook her head.

"It doesn't matter. Everything in our lives will be the

150

same one hour from now whether you win or not. It really is about accomplishment."

"You win and you've accomplished something," she replied.

"No. You learn from the experience and you have acquired something of real value. Go out there with the intention of leaving the ring a better rider than when you went in."

Greer looked at him. "Keep the hat on. I've heard too much sun can make people say crazy things."

"Let's go walk the course," Lockie said and walked through the in-gate.

"Would you please do me the favor of holding my mount? I would be ever so grateful." Greer could mimic a British accent perfectly from the years spent in England as a child.

"It would be my honor, your Grace." I curtsied as she handed me the reins.

"Of course it would be. Thank you very much." She went into the ring.

Before that moment, I had no idea Greer possessed a sense of humor.

The crowd of riders and trainers walked the course then exited. Lockie gave Greer a leg-up into the saddle and she left to keep Counterpoint moving along the driveway.

"Your sister is a real piece of work," Lockie said to me.

"I know."

"Why did she rip up the ribbon?"

"You know the answer."

"Because it wasn't enough."

"That's the problem with winning, it's an inadequate replacement for feeling good enough."

Lockie took my hand. "Can we have dinner together, just the two of us?"

"You're talking about dinner already? Didn't you eat enough lunch?"

"I just want to be alone with you."

We watched the first horse take a rail down of the out fence. "In your crummy flat."

"It's a nice apartment, Tali. I'm near the horses and there's a view of the pastures."

"We can sit on the broken couch together," I said.

That entrant left the ring and another came in.

Lockie paused. "I'm not going to try to defend the couch."

"What was Rui doing with that couch to leave it like that? On second thought, I don't want to know."

"It's not long enough to . . ."

"Shh. Don't put images in my mind."

"Sleep on! Geez, Tal."

The strawberry roan had a clean round, exited to applause and a bay mare entered.

"That couch has seen fifty miles of bad road," Lockie added.

"I don't want to know what the couch has seen. Ugh."

"I did a horse laundry last night. We'll put down CB's clean sheet for you to sit on."

"No more sheets."

"What? Oh. You mean Derry and Greer?"

"Yes."

"What a piece of cow flop leaving me like that."

"Leaving you? Leaving Greer."

"He was always going to leave Greer."

"He wasn't going to stay with us either."

"It was business. He should have said something."

"He managed to give Greer the brush-off. Bye bye . . . buffie? Something."

"Bitta fluff."

"How do you know that?"

"I spent a spring in Ireland a couple years ago. It's not entirely complimentary."

"Figures."

"You didn't say yes."

"To what?"

"To spending time on my broken couch."

"Yes. Do you really feel okay?"

Lockie nodded.

Greer's number was called and she appeared at the gate.

"I hope you've been watching the other horses go," Lockie said.

"Of course. Winning may not be everything but losing is nothing," she replied and trotted into the ring.

Lockie raised his hand. "There's the whole history of human endeavor in a nutshell."

Greer didn't bother to circle, she just made a bee-line for the first fence, passing through the laser timer. Counterpoint took the plain rails and they made the turn to the vertical double which she took to the right side instead of in the middle as everyone before her had. It was onto the rolltop.

"I told her to take that in six strides and she got it in five," Lockie said as Greer galloped to the top of the ring and made the turn down the diagonal to take the line of three fences.

Counterpoint did a flying change as they made the sharp turn to the left for the seventh fence then stretched out along the rail to take the in and out. Continuing on, she found the line between the fourth and fifth fences to take the hogsback, did another change coming off that and raced for the last two fences on the rail.

There was loud applause as Greer left the ring and I was glad to see her lean over to pat Counterpoint's neck. As we neared her, Greer dismounted and ran up her irons.

"What are you doing? There could be a jump-off," Lockie reminded her.

"I made it count so we all wouldn't have to go through that."

I wanted to say to him "don't try to figure her out" but didn't.

Greer began unbuckling the girth. "Would you hang onto the saddle, Tal?"

"You have another class," I said.

"I want to go home."

"Why?"

Greer looked at Lockie. "He doesn't feel well."

"I feel fine and staying for the next class is no problem."

"And leaving is no problem," Greer replied.

"You'll take the ami-owner jumper championship if you win this class and the next."

She looked at him for a moment. "The ribbons are really substandard. You saw how the other one fell apart."

"Okay. We'll go home."

I took the saddle off Counterpoint's back and Greer walked him away to cool down.

"Just be glad she's not screaming at us," I said shifting the saddle in my arms as we watched the other contestants do their rounds. A few minutes later, Greer's number was called and she entered the ring to be presented with another blue ribbon. I made a mental note to take it from her before she destroyed this one, too.

She led Counterpoint from the ring, the ribbon on his browband waving slightly in the breeze. "So."

"That's your last schooling show," Lockie told her.

"Good. I was bored."

"You won't be after this."

"Then it'll be the first time in my life I'm not," Greer said as she led Counterpoint back to the trailer.

~ 14 ~

We talked about dinner on the way home. Take-out, but what? Pizza or Chinese or buffalo burgers from the Grill Girl in town? It would be so early when we finished our chores and cleaned up, I suggested we eat by the stream. Lockie said he wasn't going to carry pizza that far, what was wrong with eating at the picnic bench behind the barn if we had to eat outside with the bugs.

"You choose. Next time I'll choose," I said. "Truthfully, how did Greer do?"

"She's found her niche in life and the horse that can do everything she needs. I hope she can keep focused on it for her sake."

"She was better today."

"If shredding her ribbon is a sign that Greer's becoming

more socialized, then you are much more of an optimist than I am."

"She gave you her hat to wear. She doesn't let people wear her clothes."

"As an upside to her, she is very pretty."

"Greer's always been the beautiful daughter."

"Tali, I'm not comparing the two of you."

"I'm just stating a fact. She's very difficult to ignore like an over-bright light bulb glaring into your eyes. Her mother, Victoria, is an ageless beauty, and works at it, going to spas and Swiss clinics continually."

"Speaking of clinics, I'm going to one in October."

"So you don't feel well. You didn't think to tell me?"

"Tali, quit it. It's a dressage clinic with Ula Grahn and I'll be away about three days. I'll stay with Marilyn Theissen."

We had bought CB from the Theissens who lived in Pennsylvania.

"Why do you want to attend a clinic?"

"Everyone needs to work with someone who sees you with fresh eyes."

"Please be careful."

"You know I am."

Did I know that?

Lockie turned the van slowly into the driveway of the farm. Greer had arrived ahead of us and was waiting at the barn to take Counterpoint into the wash stall and clean him after a day when he barely broke a sweat.

CB nickered to me as I came down the aisle. "You just think I'm going to produce a carrot for you." He made his gimme face, stretching his neck, looking pathetic so I took a carrot from my tote bag and broke it into a couple pieces for him.

"I know this is the last thing you want to hear," Lockie started as he put his hand on CB's neck. "You need to step-up the training for the hunter pace, both of you."

"I know. Would you come with me?"

"That would involve me riding." Lockie was smiling.

"You do when I'm not looking anyway."

"I do." He put his hand behind my neck, drew me to him and kissed me lightly. "Yes. I will ride with you a couple times a week."

I put my arms around him. "Lockie."

"Yes, I'll be careful."

"No."

"No I won't be?"

"It's not what I meant." I paused. The comfort radiated from him like the setting sun at the end of a perfect summer day. "Just Lockie."

"Silly Filly. Everything is going to be okay."

My phone started ringing.

"Get it. We have to get ready to go forage for some food anyway."

I clicked on the phone. "What?"

"Whatever you two are doing down there, come up to the house for the big surprise." Greer hung up.

* * *

Three minutes later, we walked into the kitchen.

"Gram!" I said in shock.

Greer was laughing off to the side of the room.

My grandmother embraced me, kissed me, then held me at arm's length. "Look at you. How big you've grown!"

I saw Greer mouthing the words at the same time.

My father and grandfather entered just as Jules was plating bite-sized appetizers.

"My two favorite girls," my grandfather said as he gave me a kiss.

"Hi. This is a surprise," I managed to say.

Since my grandparents lived in North Carolina, we only saw them a few times a year. After my grandfather retired, quite young and full of it, they traveled and caroused their way around the world and elsewhere. The last visit we had was when they were on their way to boat down the Danube in the spring.

Jules arrived with the plate and gave me a nudge.

"Right. Miri and Shay Swope, this is Lockie Malone our trainer. Lockie, these are my grandparents who live in North Carolina and whom we rarely see."

Lockie and my grandparents shook hands. "It's a pleasure to meet you and see where Greer and Talia got their exceedingly fine genes."

My grandfather laughed.

My father laughed.

Greer would have been doubled over if she didn't have so much practice with them. We didn't agree on much but Greer and I did share the embarrassment of these shock and awe visits during which we were practically pushed up against a doorway to measure how much we had grown since last time.

"We just returned from New Zealand. It's winter there, you know."

"It's such a lovely country," my grandmother said.

"And the water goes down the drain in the opposite direction," Greer added.

My grandmother looked at me. "Is that true?"

"Yes, it is."

"It always went straight down when I was watching."

"I think it's less noticeable in a sink and you probably need to look at a bathtub," Lockie said.

"I have nothing to do besides standing there watching water drain?"

"That's true, Mom, you're very busy overseeing your charities and we have a dinner reservation," my father said.

"We're going out?"

My grandfather put his arm around my shoulder and squeezed me to him so tightly I that was almost lifted off my feet. Greer was laughing safely from the other side of the table.

"The Silas Turnbull Inn," my father replied.

It was one of the oldest taverns in the state and famous for its fine dining. We rarely went there because neither Greer nor I wanted to be bored to death before the food was served.

"It was so nice to meet you, Mr. and Mrs. Swope. Maybe I'll see you tomorrow. If not, have a nice trip to wherever you're going." Lockie began to turn for the door and Jules grabbed his arm.

"We're all going out to eat," Jules said.

Greer didn't bother holding in her laughter.

* * *

Four hours later, on the sagging, horrible couch, I snuggled up against Lockie and that made the whole somnolence-inducing evening worthwhile.

We had listened to stock market talk, brass fittings talk, vacation talk, then back to finance, food and of course, Greer's stellar performance of the day. I spent more time trying not to yawn than following anything discussed.

"I'm sorry." I put my hand on his chest and felt his warmth on my skin.

"For what?" Gently, Lockie stroked my head.

"You must have been so bored."

"By your grandparents? Not at all. Your grandfather

took the business he inherited and rescued it. They teach about what he did in business schools. If he's gallivanting around the world now, he deserves it. He must have put in twenty-six hour days for years."

"Is that why we're all screwed up?"

"You're not, and Greer? She's just very spirited."

"That's letting her off the hook."

"She'll get with the program eventually."

"You're sure?"

"Yes, because I know her father and now her grandparents. Do you know how many businesses are lost due to mismanagement? Ten years of bad decisions long before you were born and you wouldn't be living at this wonderful farm. Your grandfather did that for you.

"I read about Clarence Mackay. He lost the fortune he inherited. All the family's art treasures were sold at auction, pieces went to museums and collectors all over the world and then the bulldozers came and razed the mansion. Ticky tacky boxes were built on the site."

"My mother used to sing that song to me."

"I'll bet she did. You're lucky. That's it. Instead of Silly I should call you Lucky."

"I don't feel lucky very often."

"Start." Lockie brushed a kiss across my skin.

"I'm lucky right now. I'm sitting with you on this sofa, even if it should be burned for Walpurgis Night."

"When?"

"It was in a book my mother read to me. On the night of April 30 in Northern Europe they would have a huge festival with dancing and bonfires to celebrate the arrival of spring."

"We don't have springs in this couch," Lockie commented.

"No, and by the end of the year your house will be finished. I hope that means you're staying."

"I'll think about it," Lockie teased.

I squeezed his side.

"Someday you may change your mind about me living here."

"Someday a large asteroid might hit the planet and wipe out life as we know it," I replied.

"Good point. We should stock up on freeze dried meals in case."

"If we're all dead, why do we need a year's worth of dried scrambled eggs?" I asked.

"Plan on surviving the asteroid strike, Tali."

I shook my head.

"If you don't survive, who will be around to nag me to take better care of myself?"

"You'll find someone," I replied.

"You said everyone would be wiped out."

"You haven't seen many sci-fi movies. There are always communities of survivors like in Australia."

"And Montana."

"There you go. When the asteroid hits, start walking," I advised him.

His phone began ringing. "I have to get this. It's probably about Memento." Lockie clicked on his cell phone. "Lockie Malone. Oh. Uh huh. Yeah. No problem. See you." He clicked off the phone and reached over to put it on the end table. "You need to go back to the house, Silly."

"Why? Do you have a girl coming to spend the night?"

"No. Josh."

15

I SAT UP. "Why is Josh coming here?"

"Silly, that's Josh's business."

"Why are you suddenly best friends?"

"Go to back the house and go to sleep. I'll see you in the morning." Lockie kissed me.

"I wanted to snuggle on the couch."

"So did I. We'll snuggle tomorrow. Tonight I snuggle with Josh."

"Lockie."

"I'm kidding. He's not my type. I'm doing this because he was important to you."

I sighed. "How am I supposed to go home after you say something like that?"

"I wanted to make it as hard as I could on you."

"You succeeded."

* * *

When I reached my bedroom, I didn't look out the window to see when Josh drove in. After reading for a couple hours, I finally felt sleepy, turned off the light and slid down between the sheets. Even though I had taken a shower, it was as if I could still smell the scent of Lockie on my skin. I rolled over and fell asleep.

* * *

In the morning, I went to the barn without having breakfast and saw Josh's car was still there. Entering the barn, Pavel was beginning to feed the horses.

"Lockie's not down yet?" I asked.

"I haven't seen him," Pavel answered as he wheeled the cart down the aisle containing the large buckets of grain being doled out to each horse as per the instructions Lockie left on each stall door.

Taking a small bucket, I scooped up CB's breakfast and brought it to him while he talked to me the entire time.

I could barely get it into the feed tub with his head in the way. "Yes, you're starving to death." I ran my hand down his barrel. "I can feel every rib. Why, you're all skin and bones, covered by layers of fat and rock hard muscle.

167

I'll throw you some hay if you can manage to wait that long."

I closed the stall door, headed to the hay room and hoisted several large bales of fragrant second cutting onto the hay cart. Most of the horses would eat all the hay they wanted while they were in their stalls. Some were on more of a diet than that, Butch, for one, now that he was retired and out to pasture much of the time. Most veterinarians would say the best feed was hay but depending on their work and health, all our horses received rations of grain and some supplements.

As I wheeled the cart onto the aisle, I nearly bumped into Josh. "Hi."

It was as though he was trying to get past me but I still got a good look at him.

"What happened to you?"

Josh wouldn't lift his face to me.

"He had a little too much to drink and ran into a door," Lockie said. "Don't do that again, Josh."

"No, I won't. Thanks, Lockie. See you, Tal." Josh practically ran down the aisle.

I turned to Lockie. "There's a scuff mark on his cheekbone, he's getting a black eye and on the other side of his face, there's a bruise. Tell me how you do that by running your face into a door."

"If Josh wanted you to know, he'd tell you."

"Why is he telling you?"

Lockie looked at me as though I already knew the answer.

"Do I need to be worried about him?"

"You don't need to be worried about anything except going to the house and having breakfast with me. Then we have horses to exercise, the crew is coming to finish up the outside course and this afternoon someone is coming to look at Memento."

"I'm worried about Josh," I admitted as we left the barn.

"That's why he was trying to sneak out. Josh cares about you and wanted to subvert your usual over-reaction."

Over-reaction? "I always told him 'don't go to gay bars'."

"Talia, stop. He's a man. Josh has to make these decisions for himself."

"Legally, he's not. At his age, it's against the law."

"So are a lot of things but people do them anyway."

"You mix alcohol with . . ."

We walked up the driveway together and, smiling, he let me struggle.

"This is becoming such a fascinating conversation that I can hardly wait to see how you're going to extricate yourself from the hole you're digging."

"Desires . . ."

"Desires?" Lockie put his arm around my shoulders and squeezed me.

"Josh looks like an adult and people . . .drunk people could mistake him for someone who . . ."

"Yes?"

"Wants the same thing they do."

Lockie opened the kitchen door for me. "You are so sweet."

"There's nothing sweet about it."

"Yes, you achieved a new level of adorableness in trying to avoid saying certain words."

"What words is she avoiding?" Jules asked as she cut up some honeydew melon.

"Never mind." I went to the stove.

"All right then. What do you want for breakfast," she asked me. "What words?" Jules asked Lockie.

"Josh stayed with Lockie last night."

Jules inhaled audibly. "Why?"

"That's what this is about. Lockie won't say and when I saw Josh just now his face was bruised. Both sides. That would make the cover story that he ran into a door a complete fabrication."

"That does sound serious," Jules said.

"It is."

"Josh wants to deal with his life in his own way. Just the way you want to deal with your life, Tal, and the way I want to deal with mine."

"No, you're not allowed to deal with your life in the way you choose," I said pouring him a mug of hot water and plopping a tea bag into it.

"How did I know that?" He asked sitting at the table.

"We're having brunch later for your grandparents, Tal. Maybe you want to wait for that meal and have something to tide you over right now."

"I have work at the barn all morning."

"Dodged the bullet on that one," Jules said with a wink as she handed me two bowls full of melon and berries.

Greer entered the kitchen dressed in her everyday breeches.

"Hi," I said, contemplating what caused her to be doing awake and conscious so early.

"Hi," she replied going to get the coffee, then found her place at the table. "I know we don't have anything on the schedule for today, Lockie, but would it be possible to have a session on Spare this morning?"

Jules and I exchanged a look. Something had happened to Greer overnight and a pod person had been exchanged for the standard issue.

"Yes. Tali is riding CB this morning on the flat. You may join her and then we can do some work over fences."

I waited for the explosion.

"Thank you," Greer replied.

"Would you like to ride Memento this afternoon for some buyers coming to look at him?"

Greer was baffled. "Me?"

"He's an equitation horse and you're an extremely accomplished equitation rider. You'd show him to his best advantage."

171

She hesitated for a second. "Yes."

Another entity really had walked into her body overnight and I began to wonder if we needed to perform an exorcism on her or if we should just accept the new personality and forget Greer ever existed.

"If I'm back in time from my lunch date," Greer added.

The poles hadn't shifted after all. Earth was safe on its axis.

"Tali will be here, she'll ride," Lockie replied and finished his tea.

Greer glanced at me. I nodded.

"I'll cancel lunch. If it will make you happy."

"It would," Lockie said pushing back from the table. "I'd like to see more of you at the barn."

"You're just saying that."

"No, I could use another rider. Come along with us and we'll have the lesson."

* * *

We worked for a half hour on suppleness. Of the four of us, only CB possessed it in quantity. Spare was too green to be supple, Greer was too impatient and I felt incompetent.

Butch and I had been at the same level and, in no stretch of the imagination, would that be considered the fast lane. We did what was required to get by, and up until Lockie had arrived, that was sufficient. Now the reality was evident. I knew far less than CB and that would probably always be true. If we weren't able to perform the exercises, it was my fault.

"Walk," Lockie said from the middle of the arena. "Talia, what's wrong?"

I had missed the turn off the wall because all I could think of was Josh and how his face looked like a meat tenderizer had been applied to it.

Why was he going to Lockie who he barely knew? Why didn't he come to me if he was in trouble? It was a given that Josh couldn't go home looking the way he did, but there were other school friends.

Of course, maybe he didn't want them to know either. Josh could have gone to Rogers' house but her parents were friends with the Standishes. If they saw Josh with a black eye, that fact wouldn't remain a secret for long.

This was why I had always advised Josh to be cautious about where he went. I never felt he understood what it was like to live in a city, or to meet up with street-wise tough guys.

Everyone Josh knew was like him and unfortunately, being a Standish had sheltered him from reality. Attending The Briar School didn't prepare him for how he might be treated elsewhere.

A little taller than I was, Josh was slender and lithe but not as physical. My strength had developed from years being in the barn lifting heavy bales of hay, moving jumps and dealing with horses that used their weight and muscle against me. Because he had no choice, Josh played soccer at school and did some swimming at home. He didn't make any pretense of being a jock. If a couple guys who spent every spare minute at the gym decided to pick a fight with the cutie from the country, there was no question how it would turn out.

I was certain that was what happened to Josh and he was too embarrassed to reveal the truth to me.

Perhaps it was my fault and Lockie was right. I should keep my concern for everyone's safety to myself but instead my worries became their white noise. Under those conditions, Josh could have found it impossible to come to me, so the only person he had to turn to in his time of need was Lockie who was practically a stranger.

Still, my misgivings were proven all too accurate and Josh's couldn't take care of himself in a dicey situation. Making his own mistakes was not a praiseworthy achievement and it put everyone who cared about Josh in a position to stand idly by while he was hurt. For what purpose? If it was to learn by experience, being assaulted was one heck of lesson.

"Talia," Lockie called to me as I sat there on the track between the K and E positions. "Are you still with us?"

I turned to him and thought how much he knew and how little I knew.

"Maybe I'm not cut out to be a dressage rider."

"Oh, for pity's sake," Greer groaned from across the arena.

"Okay. You're done for the day. After you've taken care of him, turn CB out in the paddock. Greer, walk not hack, over the cavelletti." Lockie pointed to the rails on the arena floor. "Let Spare understand what's being asked of him. This is still work."

I rode CB to the middle of the ring and dismounted next to Lockie.

"Are you angry with me?"

"No," he replied while watching Greer on the track.

"Disappointed?" I followed Lockie to the end of the cavelletti where he lowered the jump to the floor.

"Stop obsessing about Josh."

"I knew something was going to happen."

Lockie took a step closer to me and put his hand on my arm. "You didn't know. You feared it would. Just because you think something, doesn't cause it to happen. That's not your super power."

"Hello. I'm still here," Greer called from across the arena. "Put her on the couch and psychoanalyze her after my lesson."

"I wish I had the power to keep everyone safe . . ."

CB rested his chin on my shoulder and his head weighed a ton. I looped my arm around his face.

"No one has that power," Lockie said.

"If I tried harder . . ."

"You're at a hundred percent capacity now. Why don't you use your real super power?"

"What's that?"

"You don't need to do anything else besides caring about us and you're very good at it."

"Kiss him so I can finish the lesson!" Greer shouted at us.

I kissed Lockie on the cheek.

"That's it? What is the matter with you? Do you need me to show you how it's done?"

"You've shown me," I replied as I led CB from the indoor to the sound of her laughter.

* * *

That evening, my grandparents long gone, Greer out with her friends, my father away and Jules inside watching *So You Think You Can Cook*, Lockie and I sat together on the terrace.

"I start school tomorrow."

"I thought it was next week."

"Moving it up was a suggestion from my father," I replied and we both knew the weight his suggestions carried.

"It won't be that much different than the way things are now. You'll still be here."

The crickets were creating a nocturnal symphony as I reclined against his chest and felt him kiss the top of my head.

~ 16 ~

TWO WEEKS LATER, I had done more schoolwork than any semester I could remember and The Briar School was a prep school not a country club. The history course Amanda had set for me was intensive. We had started with *The Declaration of Independence* and it wasn't enough to read the words, I had to understand the document and its place in the founding of America.

It was as though we were looking at those years through a microscope. At first, I was lost in a distant time with no map, but Amanda had the ability to bring life to the pages and I began to look forward to the hours spent with her.

Then I'd race to the barn and fit all my riding into the rest of the day. Sometimes I would find Greer there already, having left school early. If she had done that during the spring, Greer would have made it to the Medal and the Maclay.

I suspected she knew that but never mentioned it.

* * *

The phone in the tack room rang.

"Get that, will you, Tal?" Lockie called. He was crouched on the aisle wrapping Counterpoint's legs.

I picked up the receiver. "Bittersweet Farm."

"Bad news, Tal," Jules said. "Rogers just got hit in the head with a field hockey stick."

I felt the shockwave course through me. "Is she okay?"

Lockie came into the tack room. "Is who okay?"

"Rogers," I said to him.

"She has a concussion. She's staying overnight at the hospital," Jules replied.

"Thanks," I said and hung up. "This is what happens when you take phys. ed. in school. You get hurt."

"Who are we talking about?"

"Someone clubbed Rogers during field hockey and she's at the hospital."

"We'll go see her."

An hour later, we walked into Rogers' room where her left eye was swollen shut and there were butterfly stitches across her temple. She looked appallingly bad.

"Rogers, how do you feel?" I handed her the bouquet of flowers we had picked up at the local market. It wasn't an impressive floral display but with the baby's breath, carnations and a couple ferns, it got the point across.

Rogers punched the bed with her hand. "I have a splitting headache, I can't see out of one eye and they won't let me ride in the hunter pace!"

"That's not important," Lockie said as he went around to the other side of her bed, while I sat on the edge.

"It is!"

"Don't cry," I said. "It'll just make you feel worse and the tears will get backed up behind your eyelid and cause your brain to flood."

"Don't try to make me feel better! This is a catastrophe!"

"Rogers. It's a hunter pace," Lockie said. "We'll go to another one. There's one in South Salem, there's one in Fairfield County. Golden's Bridge holds one each year. You can ride in all of them."

I gave Lockie a warning glance.

"This was our hunter pace. I wanted . . ."

"You don't have anything to prove to those people."

"I do." Tears began spilling onto her pink cheeks. "They always made me ride at the back of the field."

"They always make the juniors ride there," I replied.

"No. Anne St. Phalle always rode behind the master."

"She's French royalty or something, isn't she?"

"That's a new one on me, I never consorted with a princess," Lockie commented. "Or have I?"

"Neither did I! She wouldn't talk to a peasant like me," Rogers retorted.

He patted her shoulder. "Rest. Let your parents spoil you, eat ice cream and fancy chocolates all day long. In another week or so, we'll pick up where we left off."

"Field hockey. How does learning that improve my life?" Rogers wailed paying no attention to anything Lockie said.

"It's not for you future like math, it's for your health now. It's supposed to be good for you."

"Bull. You hated gym, too."

I sure had.

* * *

In the hospital parking lot, I got into the truck and closed the door. "That's a relief."

Lockie got in the passenger side. "What is?"

"Now I don't have to ride in the hunter pace."

"Who says?"

"You go as a team. I just lost my team mate," I replied, heading the truck toward home.

"I'll take Rogers' place."

I almost stomped on the brake. "No, you won't."

"I don't want to fight with you about this."

"We agree then. I'm not going to fight with you and I won't ride with you. You aren't supposed to jump. A hunter pace entails jumping."

"Not that much."

"Lockie, you agreed to these terms weeks ago. My father told me not to nag and I haven't. Your part of the deal was to stay on the flat."

"Well . . ."

I turned the truck into the farm driveway. "Oh my God. You've been riding the outside course, haven't you?"

"I had to try it out."

"I'm not talking to you again until I can speak without swearing."

"Talia, it's not that big of a deal."

I didn't say anything.

"You're fighting with me." Lockie got out of the truck. "I'm tougher than you are." He closed the door with more force than was required.

He was right about one thing. He was tougher than I was.

* * *

The chasm between us was unbearable. The two hours I stayed in my room made me feel as though I couldn't breathe.

Once when I had been much younger and riding Butch on the road, something had spooked him. Not being a very good rider then, I came off and hit the pavement hard. It seemed like an eternity before my lungs would work, then I gasped for air as if I had been too long under water.

This situation was like that. That's how he was tougher

than I was because I knew he didn't feel the same way now. It wasn't that he didn't have emotions, it was that I had too many. They controlled me instead of the other way around. I didn't stop at feeling things deeply, I felt everything too acutely.

Every event could become a crisis because that's what I had learned. I couldn't do enough to hold the world together.

It was easy for Lockie to say I should just care about those around me. I couldn't just care because that wasn't enough. The emotion had to become an action or it didn't count.

The best way to do this often eluded me, and the right words were like a bizarre list on a treasure hunt, but I was convinced any attempt was better than none.

When I didn't come downstairs for dinner, there was a knock at my door.

"Yes?"

"May I come in?" My father asked.

"Yes."

He stepped into my room wearing a nice blue shirt and trousers. "Dinner is a family meal and you should be there."

"I'm not good company right now."

"I don't like how you're behaving. It's unnecessary and you're a better person than this."

"Do you know that he wants to ride in the hunter pace in place of Rogers? The doctors wouldn't sanction that."

"Lockie has . . ."

"I don't want to hear about people making their own decisions when they're wrong."

"That's not what I was going to say even if it is the truth. Don't you think I would have flown your mother to any clinic in the world for medical treatment? I found an institute in France where they are doing research. It might have bought her time. Did you know that?"

"No."

"It's true. She decided to stay home with you. I tried to persuade her that there was the possibility of an extended future if we made the trip to Europe but she said no."

"Why?"

"It was about the quality of her life but it was more about being allowed to keep her dignity. She didn't want to feel pathetic."

"She was never that."

"No, she never was and I wouldn't take that self-regard from her, even if it might have meant an extra six months. Don't take Lockie's dignity away. Besides, we have a partial solution and if you grace us with your presence, you'll see that."

My father left the room. I changed and went downstairs to find everyone at the table, including Greer. I pulled out my chair next to Lockie and sat down.

"Wonderful. We're all here."

"Why does everything have to be high drama with her?" Greer asked.

"Look who's talking," I replied.

"You're both grounded," my father said evenly.

"What?" Greer protested. "What did I do?"

"You can't ground me, I never go anywhere," I replied.

My father regarded both of us seriously. "That's true. I'll have to think of something else."

Jules laughed.

"I'm glad you find this amusing," Greer said to her.

Jules shrugged.

"Enough. I have a present for Lockie."

"Why does he get a present? Is it his birthday?" Greer asked.

"You may have a present, too, very soon," my father said as he leaned over and lifted a box from the floor. He handed it to Jules who passed it to Lockie.

At first Lockie seemed confused, then he began to smile.

"Open it," Greer said.

Lockie lifted the lid.

"It's the prototype," my father said as Lockie removed the helmet from the packing material.

"A helmet."

Greer seemed to be disappointed it wasn't something she'd want.

Lockie turned it over to look inside then held it up for me to see.

It looked like my helmet inside. "So?"

"The difference is the material we used, not the construction of the shell or the harness. That's the same as any helmet. It would have been impossible to get a prototype made and also create a completely new helmet quickly enough."

"Will this protect a rider's head more than any other helmet?" Jules asked.

"No," my father replied.

"Then what is this all about?" Greer asked in exasperation.

"We believe it will protect the brain more efficiently. Further testing needs to be done but all indications are that this helmet will be an improvement in safety."

Lockie put the helmet on and it fit him perfectly.

"And in our stable colors," I said because I didn't know what else to say.

"All right. Let's have dinner," Jules said enthusiastically.

Lockie took off his new helmet and replaced it in the box.

I felt as though Lockie had just been given a carte blanche to take as many risks as he desired.

The meal was wonderful, dessert was delicious, and I had no appetite. No one seemed to notice as they ate heartily and I picked.

The only person I ever fought with was Greer and I didn't care very much if we never spoke to each other again.

With Lockie, I cared. Since I told him I wasn't going to speak to him, there was no way of knowing if he'd attempt talking to me first.

I didn't know how to bridge the gap I created. Apologizing would be a good start, but the truth was I still didn't want him to ride and the new helmet hadn't changed that. I couldn't envision a scenario where Lockie went to a doctor's appointment, showed them the helmet and their response was "Hallelujah! Do whatever you want!"

The truth was also that I wished I had known earlier how hard my father had tried to press my mother into accepting new medical treatments and why he had finally submitted to her judgment. I considered it the right, although difficult, decision and in that, I took after my father. It would not have made me happy to see her reduced to begging for a few more days even if it had meant more time together.

There does come a point where accepting reality is the sensible thing to do.

What was sensible now? Giving in was inevitable because Lockie did have a stronger will than I did. That didn't make me happy to admit since I had spent most of my life trying to be in control and all I had been doing was flailing against fate.

When dinner was finished, Greer and my father went off in separate directions and Jules went to the kitchen.

There was a deep silence between us that forced me to

say something. "I'm not going to stop being concerned about you. The helmet doesn't change that," I said, not looking at him.

"Fair enough. You'll ride with me on the hunter pace?"

"I'm riding with you, you're not riding with me?"

"If you want to put it like that."

"Do you know what position this puts me in?"

"Untenable if you don't give in."

I thought for a long moment because the choice was important. "You win."

"It's not about winning, it's about losing gracefully." Lockie smiled. "Stay with me tonight. You can, for the first and only time, spend as long as you like telling me what a bastard I am."

I looked at him and shook my head. "That's not how I feel."

~ 17 ~

WE LAY ON HIS BED and Lockie reached over to turn off the light. While not an unpleasant scent, I could smell the hay on the other side of the wall. It was as close to living in a barn as it was possible to get without actually living in a barn.

The frame of his cottage was already raised in the front field near the road. Every day CB and I would hack down the driveway to check on the progress as I could barely wait for him to be able to move. It would be comfortable, fresh and clean there. He would have new furniture or very old furniture as Jules kept telling me we had to go antiquing to furnish the carriage house. She seemed to be having a wonderful time picking out paint, appliances and floor coverings.

This would be Lockie's first home of his own, even if it was on our property. He had always been a transient, living at one farm or another, most of the time having no possessions other than his clothes, his tack, his truck and his trailer. In the carriage house, he would have closets, drawers, bookcases, a desk and a good couch. Lockie could cease being a vagabond.

"So tell me off, Talia."

I reached for his hand.

"You must have been very angry with me."

"Scared for you. Yes, and angry that you would take chances."

"If I didn't have the accident, would you still be so concerned about me?"

"Of course. Your accident just puts it into sharper focus."

Lockie squeezed my hand. "I'm grateful."

"But?"

"No but."

He was grateful because I cared about him? I didn't know what to say next but it made me wish that each moment we had could be stretched to the horizon without breaking.

"If you're not going to yell at me, try to sleep. We have a long trip to take tomorrow."

"I can't go, I have school."

"Amanda gave you the day off, it's that important."

"Where are we going?"

"New York State."

"To look at a horse?"

Why would that get me out of school for the day?

"Trust me, Talia."

* * *

We were on the road heading west by seven, my hair still wet from my shower, not knowing any more about our destination than I did the night before. The GPS on his dashboard told him what roads to take and I was lost, never having been in this part of the state before. Soon enough it became obvious we were in the Catskills region, there were enough signs to give me a hint.

"Are you getting nervous, Silly?"

"Curious."

"Only?"

There was no point in pretending with Lockie. He read me as easily as he did any of the horses. "No."

"Don't be. This is for you."

We made another turn onto a narrow country road and drove for only a few minutes.

"You have reached your destination," the GPS told us.

Lockie slowed the truck then stopped.

I turned to him.

He lowered the sun-visor, took a photo from it and held it out in front of us.

The photograph was of my grandmother Margolin as a very young woman sitting where we were now, at the entrance to a vacation resort. The sign was gone, just the frame remained and that was falling apart. The stone bench was still there although almost obscured by an old wild rose bush.

"Why?" I asked.

He handed me the picture I had shown him months ago.

"You know."

I couldn't put it into words without tearing up and he knew it.

"Go out there and sit where she sat. I'll take your picture."

Lockie reached for his camera bag from behind the seat and opened the door.

I was frozen again between the K and E of my life.

"Get a move on, we have to get home. Horses to ride. Fences to be thrown into," he teased.

"Lockie!"

"You can't yell at me today, you missed your chance last night."

Opening the truck door, I wished I had a sundress and the oxford shoes to wear like my grandmother had on in the old photograph. In mid-stride, I paused.

"Don't cry, Talia. This is for your granddaughter. Let her see you smiling the way you can see your grandmother smiling. Someday she will hand it to a young man, the way you did to me, the way your mother did to your father and she will say 'My grandmother had a beautiful smile.'"

Lockie raised his camera. I walked to the granite slab and sat down, positioning myself in the pose my grandmother had struck. I felt as though I was looking down a narrow tube into a future so far away that I couldn't see the person looking back at me but who existed as surely as I did.

* * *

Greer was riding Spare toward the barn when we drove in. She pulled up and slid off.

Lockie got out of the truck. "Did you ride Counterpoint?"

"He's off," she replied, running up her irons.

"That's why I wrapped him last night. I hoped it was just a strain."

"Maybe it is," Greer replied. "Where did you two go?"

"Shin Creek, New York."

"What's there?"

"An old bench covered in roses."

"Sounds like fun," Greer replied without enthusiasm. "Lockie, you had a call just after lunch from some photographer in the city. Call him back."

"Did he say what it's about?"

"Dad's office gave him the number."

"Okay."

"I left it by the phone."

"Thank you, Greer," Lockie replied and went into the barn.

"How is that teacher Dad got for you?" Greer asked me.

"Amanda is brilliant."

"Do you like being home-schooled?"

"So far. It's the one-on-one attention that makes everything move faster but there's a lot more work."

"You always did like reading," Greer replied.

"Yes. It helped me forget where I was."

"You just don't know how to make the best of a bad situation, do you?"

I shrugged. "I'm learning."

By the time I reached CB's stall to give him a handful of grain, Lockie was leaving the tack room.

"You need a shave," I said.

Lockie put his hand on his face to check.

I laughed. "I'm talking to CB."

His whiskers were prickly on my skin as he closed his lips around the oats.

"We have an unusual event scheduled here for tomorrow," Lockie announced.

"I'm breathless with suspense," Greer said, her voice reeking of ennui, as she led Spare to the wash stall.

"If boredom threatens, then you can go off to Millbrook and be with your friends," Lockie replied. "I'm sure you have no interest in fashion shoots."

"Excuse me?"

"Maurizio Bevelaqua is a top photographer for some magazine I never heard of and can't remember what he said now. They're bringing the crew and using the farm as a set."

"Why?" Greer asked standing in the doorway with the hose in her hand.

"Because we're picturesque," Lockie replied. "We're an iconic horse farm."

Greer made a face and went back to Spare.

"No, really, why?"

"That is the reason. Because they need the landed gentry look."

"What audience is that?"

"I have no clue. There will be a model and they're bringing their equipment, reflectors and what all they need to accomplish this project."

"Why does it have to be tomorrow?"

"Because the weather is going to be beautiful tomorrow but it's going to rain later in the week."

"You're kidding, right?"

"No, that's the weather forecast as of this morning," Lockie said as he went to Wingspread's stall.

"The ground is going to be wet for the hunter pace?"

"If it rains it will be."

"No. I don't like it."

"Come here."

I stepped closer to him and he kissed me. "It will be fine. We'll put studs in their shoes."

When he arrived at the farm, Lockie had the farrier switch most of the horses over to shoes that would take studs. They were used to give better traction while riding cross-country. Since neither Greer nor I competed in cross-country events before Lockie became our trainer, we had never used studs.

"Did Wing have studs in his shoes the day of the accident?"

"Yes."

"So they're of no help whatsoever," I said in dismay.

Lockie laughed and kissed me again. "Tack CB and we'll get some exercise."

The way he said it made it sound like it was going to be a nothingburger workout. By the time we got back to the barn, I could barely stand up my legs were so tired.

"The hunter pace is going to be tough for you," Lockie said dismounting and flipping his irons over the saddle.

"Hang on. There's the hunt speed division, the give it a good shot speed division and the Sunday stroll speed division."

"That's not the way I would describe the event but if you would like to think of it in those terms, be my guest."

"Why can't we just hack our way through the countryside?"

"Because no."

There was no point discussing it further. "All right."

Lockie turned to me quickly. "Did I hear that correctly? You said all right?"

"Yes. And make a big fuss about it so I'm well and truly embarrassed."

He stopped at the entrance to the barn. "Is that what you think, that if you give in, it's a sign of weakness?"

I thought for a moment. "Yes."

"Life is really hard for you then," he said and continued into the barn.

"Lockie?"

"You don't have to fight for everything. I'm not trying to put one over on you. All it's about is a hunter pace."

I started to refute that.

"No, Tali. There's no deeper significance to it than that. Choose your battles more wisely." Lockie slipped Wing's bridle off and exchanged it for his halter. "Besides, I really am here to help you."

"Brother, are you wasting your time, Greer said as she walked past us.

"I'm here to help you, too," he called after her.

Greer shrugged.

— 18 —

JUST AFTER I FINISHED the barn chores and was headed back to the house for my lessons with Amanda, four large SUV's and a rental truck with New York plates came down the driveway. While I would have liked to watch the proceedings, I couldn't.

Jules was working on the marble countertop rolling out pastry when I reached the kitchen. "There's a mug of tea in the microwave for you. Just heat it up."

"Do you always think of everything," I asked pressing the keypad.

"No. I forgot parsley at the market."

The bell dinged and I opened the door for my tea.

"Amanda's waiting for you. You'll see the stick figure models later."

"Or I'll get lucky and it'll be over by the time I get back to the barn," I said on my way to the den.

* * *

I wasn't lucky because nearly four hours later they were still setting up, rushing back and forth, the photographer calling out orders and people were standing near the catering truck, something that had appeared out of nowhere. A motor home had arrived and was parked blocking the gate to the north field.

In the barn, Lockie was on the aisle wrapping a sales pony's legs for shipping to a sweet young girl in New Jersey.

Crouching next to him, I kissed his cheek.

"They haven't started yet. I could have made it to the city and back by now," Lockie replied and kissed me in return.

"What the hold up?"

"The model was late."

"Did you see her?"

"No, she's hiding in the motor home being re-beautified. I think they took some shots earlier while I was in the indoor."

Lockie finished with the wrap and we stood.

"Even Greer could have been ready in that amount of time."

"I'd say we should leave but I don't know when the van's coming for this guy."

"Hey, can I have some help out here?" A man called to us from the doorway.

"What can I help you with?" Lockie asked.

"We need a prop horse."

"Excuse me?" I asked.

"A horse. A horse. Do you have one here?"

"Yes," Lockie replied. "What do you need a horse for?"

"To stand there and make the model look good," he said sharply as though we were stupid.

"What color horse would you like?"

"Something that doesn't clash with auburn hair."

"Coming right up," Lockie said as the man turned his back on us and rushed back to the photography site.

"He's quite rude," I commented.

"Bring CB out to them. He'll probably enjoy watching all the activity."

"I'm not letting them touch CB."

"You'll stand there and hold him."

"I'm not having my photo taken."

I hadn't had a shower or changed my clothes since I had done chores. There was no way I was being recorded for posterity looking as though I had just been dragged through a field and left to dry on the manure pile.

"Fine. Just bring him out there and see what they want."

A minute later, Lockie and I were walking to the crowd, CB looking around trying to take in everything. I was sure he didn't know what to make of it because I didn't.

We went past the motor home and there was a piece of paper on the door. "Ceallaigh" had been printed on it with a wide tip marking pen.

"What does that spell?" I asked him.

Lockie gave it a glance. "Looks Irish to me. I think it's pronounced Kelly."

There were a lot of letters just to say Kelly but took Lockie's word for it because I had never been to Ireland and he had.

"Is that the prop horse?" Someone shouted to us.

"Yes."

"Bring him over here, we're running late."

I didn't move. "What do you want to do with him?"

"All it has to do is stand there." A man pointed to a spot by the fence. "Can it do that?"

"He can . . ." I began.

"Don't, Tal. Let's just get them out of here with the least amount of annoyance."

I brought CB to the fence.

"Well, you have to get out of the frame," the photographer nearly snarled at me.

Leaving more slack with the lead shank, when I stepped back, CB followed me.

"Can it remain in one place?"

I pushed CB back two steps. "He's not a dog. They're not taught to sit and stay."

The model appeared. She had the kind of long, curly

hair women had in either fashion magazines or sword and sorcery movies.

"I'm glad you finally made it, Ceallaigh," the photographer said.

He pronounced it Kelly so Lockie was correct.

"Take your position by the fence again."

She turned into a statue. "Near the horse?"

"Yes."

"It's so big. What if it tramples me?"

I looked at Lockie.

"He's a big baby, you'll be fine," Lockie told her.

When Ceallaigh turned to him, it was like throwing a switch on all their auxiliary lighting. She smiled showing perfect white teeth that would have received thunderous applause at a dental convention.

"I would feel safer if you'd hold him," she said stepping closer to Lockie.

I groaned.

"It's her horse, he's crazy about her."

"Please," Ceallaigh begged him.

The van to pick up the pony made its way slowly toward the barn.

"Tal, would you take care of the pony and I'll hold CB?" Lockie asked.

I held out the lead shank to him.

"I'll make it up to you," he whispered as I passed.

"This is going to cost you, mister," I replied.

As I walked away, I thought I could hear Cellaigh cooing over him.

* * *

By the time the fashionistas left, Pavel, Tracy and I were in the middle of afternoon chores. Lockie led a food-deprived CB to his stall and he went straight to his feed tub.

"I'm hungry, too," Lockie admitted as he slid the stall door shut.

"Go up to the house and have Jules make you something."

"No, I'll wait. What needs to be done?"

"I've got it, Boss," Tracy said as she came down the aisle with the hay cart. "You worked hard all afternoon posing for photos."

I wasn't sure why the photographer decided Lockie should be in the shots because the process ground to a halt as he was primped enough to be included. As far as I was concerned, he enjoyed it too much, but it was good to see him smile. Not as good to see Ceallaigh leaning against him and looking up at him coquettishly.

Lockie and I drove up to the house where Jules was setting the table outside for dinner.

"I thought we'd take advantage of the good weather while we still have it," she said placing several large glass containers filled with water and white flower blossoms.

We went into the house and each of us helped move

utensils and plates out to the terrace. Jules brought a large bowl of salad and we sat at our places, except Greer who was still at Sabine's.

"How did the photo shoot go?" My father asked.

"They weren't underfoot," I replied. "Not much."

"Lockie joined in," Jules said.

My father looked up, surprised.

"I was the prop stable hand holding the prop horse," Lockie explained.

I pressed his knee with mine under the table.

"Thank you for helping. It's going to be a feature in *Hauteur* Magazine which has an influential readership," my father said.

"It's part of the job."

Jules served fork tender short ribs and delicate, crispy potato cakes.

We talked about selling the pony, the horses in training and eventually got around to the hunter pace.

"Are you sure it's wise for you to take Rogers' place?" My father asked.

I wasn't going to get involved since I knew Lockie had made up his mind and there was nothing that would persuade him otherwise.

"It will be little more than a trail ride," he replied.

"At speed," I added.

"Yes, cantering will be required."

"And jumping?" My father asked.

"We will avoid every jump possible," Lockie said.

"Wear your helmet and good luck to you both."

"We'll be home by lunchtime."

"Then I'll make something delicious."

"How will that be different than any other meal?" Lockie asked.

"You're so sweet," Jules said as she went to get the dessert, a gorgeous dark red summer pudding.

Jules served the berries and soaked brioche then dolloped clotted cream on top. We practically licked our bowls clean.

I expected my father to excuse himself, get up from the table and go back to his den to work. Instead, he remained seated for a long moment.

"Would anyone like to play Gin Rummy?"

Lockie looked at me for a hint.

My mother and I had played cards together often, almost every night. It was less about the game and more about being together. I had adored those evenings with her. Later on when my father was more of a presence in our lives, he would sometimes play with us.

At first uncomfortable with my father joining us since he wasn't part of the family I knew, I came to accept it as something my mother wanted. Now he was asking to revisit that time or maybe make new memories.

"It sounds like fun," Jules said with her bright smile.

"Talia?" My father asked.

I nodded. "Yes."

"I'll get the cards," Jules said as she went into the house.

"Do you play cards, Lockie?" My father asked.

"Everyone plays cards in the tack room when the day is done," he replied.

"Probably poker."

"Yes, mostly, or Twenty-one."

"Have you ever played cards in a casino?"

"No, sir. I'm not a gambler by nature," Lockie said.

I looked at him and he smiled back.

"Nor am I," my father replied.

Jules returned with a deck of cards, placed them on the table and sat across from me.

"Why don't you deal, Tali?" My father suggested.

I reached for the cards.

"You always could shuffle like a croupier."

"A hidden talent," Lockie said to me.

"I learned from my mother," I replied shuffling the cards.

"The Margolins were always gamblers," my father said.

"Were they?" Lockie asked.

"Tali's mother gambled on me," my father answered with a smile.

I began dealing.

"Are we going to keep score?" Jules asked looking at the cards dealt her.

"We never do," I said, moving cards around in my hand.

Lockie leaned over to me. "If winning doesn't count, then show me what you have."

Laughing, I hid my hand under the table. "Are you insane?"

"I'll show you mine." He turned his hand quickly to me then turned it back.

My mother would have liked him so much.

— 19 —

I SAT, HUDDLED, on CB at the gate while Lockie walked Wing in a large circle around me. It had been raining since I woke that morning and there were drops of water falling off my helmet. We were soaked and the sod at the entrance to the hunter pace had been churned to mud.

Waiting until the last possible moment, Lockie had put mud studs into the horses' shoes. They didn't look nearly long enough to me for these conditions. I didn't say that.

Rogers had held CB while I donned the body protector and fastened the helmet harness. I pulled on my gloves then she gave me a leg-up into the saddle that was already wet.

We were in a hold and the official at the gate explained that someplace on the course, the staff was rebuilding a fence. I could only imagine what had happened.

If there was any indication that Lockie had doubts about participating, I would have found an excuse to withdraw but the conditions didn't faze him. He was energized by the event.

Lockie looked like his dream come true, he was one with his horse.

For me, I had never seen anything like Lockie on Wingspread. It was an image so perfect as to be breathtaking and as enduring as a photograph.

"One minute," the starter called to us.

Lockie came up beside me. "Are you okay?"

"Yes."

He smiled. "Look at it this way. In a couple hours, you'll be able to take a hot shower."

"An upside so easily missed on a day when I can see my breath in front of me," I replied.

"Ready?" The starter raised a small flag.

I gathered my reins.

"Go."

Wingspread didn't have to be asked. Setting the tone for what I expected of the remaining five miles, he shot through the standards leaving CB and me to keep up.

The first section was through a wooded area with a wide bridle path. That opened to a large field where Wing opened up a distance between us. At the top of the hill, Lockie slowed a bit so we could catch up.

I could understand why CB wouldn't make a good cross

country horse. This wasn't his thing anymore than it was mine.

At the peak of the hill, we galloped down to the orange flag held by a scarecrow next to a fence comprised of logs. Wingspread flew over it and we followed.

After crossing a field, we jumped a red panel fence that brought us back into the woods where the path narrowed and Lockie pulled up into a trot. The ground was uneven and the path snaked through the trees. It would have been impossible to canter under these conditions.

The rain came down harder as the trail twisted and turned through the woods, with no way around some of the natural obstacles. We cantered down a hill, splashed through a stream and went up the rise.

Lockie slowed and turned in the saddle. "We're lost."

"How do you know?"

"I can feel it. We're not on the main course."

I looked at the ground. "The path is full of prints."

"When did they hunt over this land last? I think the prints are from before. They don't look fresh," Lockie replied.

"What do you want to do? Go back?"

"I don't know where we went off course."

"I thought this was supposed to be marked."

"The arrows may have fallen off the trees or stakes and we missed them."

"So?"

"Do you know this country at all?

I shook my head and rain went everywhere. "Rogers hunted out here but I never did."

"Okay. We'll keep going. This is Connecticut not Outer Mongolia. We'll get back to civilization eventually. Are you all right?"

"Yes. Are you?"

"Of course," Lockie said with a bright smile.

A moment later, we were racing through the woods, following the path of riders who had covered this recently if not that morning.

We jumped a low wooden gate that brought us to a clearing in the woods, where there was a passageway wide enough to be used by a farm vehicle.

"We have to go east," Lockie said as he pulled up.

"How do you know that?"

"It's part of my skill-set."

"Why don't we just keep going on this road or whatever it is?"

"Because we're being timed."

"We're lost. It's over for us."

"No. Did you read the details for this hunter pace? There are two courses. We may be on the alternate."

"I didn't read the flyer," I admitted.

"We have to look for a way to go east."

Lockie started trotting away so I urged CB forward.

"There we are!" He called back to me and jumped into a field.

I pulled CB to a halt and stared at Lockie who realized we were no longer behind him.

"Come on, Talia!"

"That's not a jump, it's a stock fence!"

I was looking at a four-foot tall metal gate at the entrance to a cow pasture.

"Jump it."

"No."

"It's a just vertical. CB doesn't have an opinion on it."

"No."

"You're wasting time."

The rain was hitting my face as I stared across the distance to Lockie on the other side of the fence.

"Okay. Meet me at the van. I'm finishing the event."

I glanced down the roadway. It had to lead somewhere.

I turned back to Lockie.

"Come on, Silly, you can do it."

I closed my legs on CB's sides. He took two strides and effortlessly cleared the gate. We cantered up to Wing.

Lockie leaned over and reached out to pull me to him for a kiss. "Good girl."

We galloped to the crest of the hill where we found ourselves under power lines crackling with electricity.

"We're going to get zapped," I said.

"No, we're not," Lockie replied as he let Wing gallop down the hillside.

I braced myself in the saddle, envisioning CB sliding down on his rump but we made it to the bottom and picked up tracks other riders had left earlier. Snaking through the woods, we jumped an enormous fallen tree then a chicken coop into another cow field. We galloped through the herd who regarded us with minimal interest, then jumped a stone wall into another pasture. From there we could look down on the field where there trailers were parked.

"We're unlost," Lockie called to me as he galloped down to the bottom of the hill.

There was another chicken coop to clear and we turned to the left on the obvious track to the finish line where Rogers was waiting for us.

"Cool beans!" She shouted as we cantered through the gateway and the timekeeper clocked us in. "You did so well! How was it?"

"I don't want to do it again anytime soon, okay? Get yourself another partner for Rombout or wherever the next hunter pace is."

"She did fine," Lockie said, dismounting and releasing the harness to his helmet. "I'm going to have a word with the committee and find out if we went off course or not. Would you take care of Wing, Rogers?" He held out the reins to her.

Rogers could barely answer. "Sure, yes." She put her hand reverently on Wing's neck, unable to believe the privilege given her.

I slid off CB and ran up my irons. He was covered in mud. I kissed his nose and had to wipe the horse hairs on my lips. Then because he was sweaty and itchy, CB began rubbing his head on me so hard I had to brace myself against his pushing just so he didn't knock me over.

"What's this about going off course?"

The rain was abating as I started to lead CB back to the van. "It was ugly. There was a huge stock fence going into a field . . ."

"With the high tension wires."

"Yes."

Rogers nodded as we began untacking the horses. "I've been there. On one hunt, a weekend rider from the city fell off in front of that wooden gate. She made such a fuss you would have thought she was hurt."

"Was she?"

Rogers pulled the saddle off Wing. "No."

Lockie returned to the van with a smile. "We're fine. That was the brave people course. Two teams took it—the whipper-ins and us. We came in second."

"They went faster than we did?" I was astonished.

He smiled. "They didn't have the time-outs for discussion like we did." Lockie put his arm around my shoulders and drew me to him. "You were good out there. I'm proud of you."

"If I didn't do well, if I didn't ride at all, would you still be proud of me?"

"Silly, it's not contingent upon how you ride. I'm proud of you for the person you are." He pulled me closer. "I've worked at the stables of really rich people and you know what they have? Hot tubs. We could have all go home and sit in hot water until we shrivel up."

"My grandfather didn't need a hot tub, so we don't need a hot tub," my father said as he and Jules approached.

"What are you doing here?" I asked.

They were both wearing slickers and rain boots.

"We came to watch you. Then Rogers told us there was nothing to watch," Jules said. "So we walked through tall grass up into the viewers' gallery in a field where you could see the riders pass down in the valley for about ten seconds. You never went by."

"We went in another direction," Lockie said as he went to the tack trunk for the stud kit.

"You seem to do that quite a lot," my father commented.

Lockie bent over and lifted CB's hoof to remove the mud studs. "It's a personal hallmark of mine. Is it a problem?"

"No, you fit right in with us," my father replied.

"Define us," Greer said as she appeared from the other side of the van.

"Everyone from the farm," Jules said.

Greer shook her head. "So how did you do?"

"We came in second," I told her.

"I drove all this way for nothing?"

"No," I replied walking CB up the ramp. "I appreciate you showing up whatever the reason."

"Let's go home. You can get cleaned up and we have a fantastic lunch waiting for us," Jules said. "You're invited, too, Rogers."

"Thank you!"

Lockie led Wing into the van and backed him into the stall. We lifted the ramp together and fastened it.

"Heading home," Lockie said.

We said our goodbyes, see ya laters, and Lockie and I got into the cab of the van. I was not sorry to see the end of this hunter pace but it had worked out better than expected.

Halfway to the farm, it started to rain again.

"Talia, would you spend the night with me? We can listen to the rain on the roof."

"I'll have to check my schedule."

"If you can't, that's fine, too."

I reached over and put my hand on his breeches, soaking wet and smeared with mud from the stud removal. "You looked . . .beautiful today."

"Beautiful? Isn't that what I'm supposed to say to you?" He put his hand on my hand. "Didn't I tell you it was going to be okay?"

I nodded.

For more about Bittersweet Farm, check out *Wingspread* and *Counterpoint*, available from Amazon and other other online retailers.

Bittersweet Farm 3: *Wingspread*

"Surprise!" Greer's mother says with her unannounced arrival. What Victoria Swope is doing in town is a mystery but they quickly find out and no one is pleased.

When Greer demands to be home-schooled with Talia, the lessons at Bittersweet Farm aren't restricted to dressage, cross-country, and show jumping. If the half-sisters can't get along, one of them will be sent abroad to finish high school. Unable to bear leaving the farm's trainer, Lockie Malone, or her horse, CB, Talia grits her teeth and tries to move forward.

It's soon obvious that everyone at the farm faces changes and challenges. Solving them is difficult and maybe impossible.

Bittersweet Farm 4: *Counterpoint*

Greer Swope has something to prove. But even she doesn't quite know what.

Always believing that even if she was good enough for nothing else, she was good enough on a horse. History hasn't borne that out. Now Greer's left equitation and hunter classes behind for show jumping but it won't happen overnight. It might even take the help of a new trainer. Enter Cameron Rafferty whose horse is lame, who was fired from his last job, and who wants the newest Bittersweet prospect. He's one of the top riders and he is a player. Can Greer handle her horse, Counterpoint, and Cam Rafferty, too?

Talia can only look on at what might be the latest train wreck.

Sign up for our mailing list and be among the first to know when the next Bittersweet Farm book will be out.
Send your email address to:

barbara@barbaramorgenroth.com
Note: all email addresses are kept strictly confidential

About the Author

BARBARA MORGENROTH was born in New York City but now lives somewhere else. She got her first horse when she was eleven and rode nearly every day for many years, eventually teaching equitation and then getting involved in eventing.

Although Barbara started her writing career with tween and YA books, she wound up writing for grown-up daytime television for several years. She then wrote a couple of cookbooks and a nonfiction book on knitting, after which she returned to fiction and wrote romantic comedies.

When digital publishing became a possibility, Barbara leaped at the opportunity and has never looked back. In addition to the fifteen traditionally published books she wrote, Barbara has something in digital format to appeal to almost every reader—from the Bad Apple series and the Flash series for mature YAs, to contemporary romances like *Love in the Air* published by Amazon/Montlake, along with *Unspeakably Desirable*, *Nothing Serious*, and *Almost Breathing*.

Made in the USA
Lexington, KY
11 April 2016